The Sleepwalker

First published in 2011 by

Clockroot Books
An imprint of Interlink Publishing Group, Inc.
46 Crosby Street, Northampton, MA 01060
www.clockrootbooks.com
www.interlinkbooks.com

Grateful acknowledgment is made to *Words Without Borders*, where a
portion of this novel appeared.

Text copyright © Margarita Karapanou/Kastaniotis Editions SA,
Athens, 1997, 2011
Translation copyright © Karen Emmerich, 2011

Library of Congress Cataloging-in-Publication Data
Karapanou, Margarita.
[Hypnovates. English]
The sleepwalker / by Margarita Karapanou ; translated from the Greek
by Karen Emmerich.—1st American ed.
p. cm.
ISBN 978-1-56656-838-8 (pbk.)
1. Messiah—Fiction. 2. Islands—Greece—Fiction. 3. Humorous fiction.
gsafd I. Emmerich, Karen. II. Title.
PA5622.A696H9613 2010
889'.334—dc22

2010023539

Cover art and design by Ihrie Means

Printed and bound in the United States of America

The Sleepwalker

by Margarita Karapanou

translated from the Greek by Karen Emmerich

The Sleepwalker

1

God was tired.

He had stretched out on a rock high in the sky and turned his back on the world. For the first time he felt sad, and deeply bored. He saw that his people—who in his language he called beings—were small and ridiculous, and he was gripped by an awful rage because he had created them with such love. But that had been so long ago, he couldn't remember any of it now. And now he was old. His love seemed old, too, and he was flooded with nostalgia for the passion he had felt in dreaming the World.

He remembered how he had tossed the first animals and the birds down onto the fresh earth, and had laughed proudly when he saw them running and flying. At night they slept in their caves and thought of him. And now he looked down and saw what had become of his earth. He wondered if, as he had aged, it too had aged, and so his boredom, that vast emptiness that tormented him, had become its boredom, too. He thought that perhaps he had created the earth in a moment of unlawfulness, and that's why it bore the traces of some mistake. There were moments when he felt like an outlaw from himself, moments of unspeakable, forbidden pleasure. He feared that perhaps the earth was the child of just such a moment, the child of pleasure rather than

Law. When he had created it he had still been a child himself, playing with the Universe as if unwinding a ball of yarn, a gift from some unknown Father, and measuring the depths of the heavens. Back then he'd had a dream, strange and hazy, that lasted precisely seven days: shapes with the charm of truth, faces that shone with error, graceful but aimless movements. And now he was afraid that, just for a lark, he'd made that dream into reality, and thus the earth had been formed. He had always wanted to give birth to something, there were times when he felt like a woman and wanted a child of his own, but he had been pregnant without knowing the joy of birth, and now he was terrified by the thought that he had unwillingly given birth to that dream, so imperfect and utterly sensual, the dream of his transgression.

But what did he care? All that was so long ago, so jumbled in his memory. And as his child, the earth should now be returning life to him, and the passion he had once bestowed on it, so that he, old as he now was, could sit on his rock and take pride in the earth and not be bored. But his people had annihilated him. His earth had betrayed him. And he cursed it.

So he decided to send a new God to earth, a God they would recognize and worship right from the start, a God made in their image and likeness, the kind of God they deserved. A God who would have enemies, not believers. A handsome God, since all they worshipped was beauty. A slim-hipped God, man and woman at once, since they no longer respected the Law. He ground his teeth and rose. He clutched his stomach, bent over the earth, and vomited. And the heavens opened and a great thundering groan was heard.

Manolis was sleeping on the mountain. He covered his face with his hands to shield it from the thick, putrid liquid that was pounding down on the bushes and grass. But as soon as he opened his eyes, he realized he had been dreaming, that vomit was rain.

He got to his feet. But he didn't see God bending over him, watching him, mouth a steaming hole, eyes two black domes. Nor did he realize that what he had experienced wasn't a dream, that the rain really was vomit, and that he had been re-baptized, Emmanuel once more.

He walked on the mountain. He had become lord and the four elements of nature obeyed him, the animals bowed their heads as he passed, the earth trembled beneath his feet, and he hadn't the slightest idea. Thus began the new Worship, and the new Law.

2

Mark woke up.

"It's morning. It's morning and I have to get up, have to pretend I'm opening my eyes, stretching, smiling cleverly at the thought of my work, brushing my teeth, making coffee."

He fell asleep again. When he opened his eyes it was dark.

"It's night. It's night and there are only two hours before I leave for Maggie's. I have to pretend I can stand it, surely I can manage two hours."

He got up, stretched, smiled, brushed his teeth, and poured a drop of coffee into a glass of vodka. There were seven glasses ready on the table: he poured them out every Monday and meant for them to last the whole week, but by Tuesday they were always empty, so for him the week ended on Tuesday. "I'll see you on Saturday," Alex would say, and when Mark showed up on Tuesday night for their poker game Alex would send him away, saying, "Go home and work."

The house was dark. The only light he turned on was the spotlight over the easel. He sat down in a chair, lit a cigarette, and looked at the painting. It was windy outside, it was February—*The worst month, because it's in the middle*, he thought. *But the middle of what?* He felt dizzy; he could hear the sea in the distance and it seemed as if the waves were clambering up over the rocks, galloping over the mountain, jumping the fences, closing in on the house, lapping at his feet. *February. The worst month of all.* Mark stood up. The wind outside seemed to be circling more and more tightly around his neck, so he grabbed another vodka and sat back down in front of the easel. The portrait had been sitting there for two years, unfinished, faceless, a slim-hipped body, one hand lifting a cigarette toward an invisible mouth. It looked like someone but he couldn't figure out who, so the portrait remained headless, though the body was finished. Actually, none of his portraits had heads—everyone said that's what made them unique, but Mark only left them that way because he always started with the feet and by the time he got to the neck he was drunk. This one, though, he wanted to finish. He picked up a brush and dabbed a bit of red onto the end of the cigarette, then drank another vodka and started running around the room, singing:

"My house is cold, my house is damp, my house is dirty, my dear lady, but tonight I want to paint your white beauty, tonight I want you, not that man who won't show me his face—sure, I often dream of boys, little boys I undress and lay out on the rug, kissing them on the mouth before I paint them, I feel such desire for those innocent, clever smiles, though this one on the easel has something terribly manly about him, I'm drunk, my dear lady, and tonight I want you,

I saw you yesterday at the bar, I was cold and you were so white and fat I wanted to fall on you and get warm, I had to grab hold of my chair to keep myself from lunging—in February I always feel the need for feminine fat, boys are for springtime. February, short days, endless darkness—I'm cold, I'm cold, so unbearably cold."

Mark wiped away his tears with the cloth he used for his brushes, picked up the last glass, and lay down.

"These past few days I've been ruled by a quiet panic. I'd like once and for all to sit on the scraps of my ass and rest."

He closed his eyes. Another day had passed. He had survived.

Luka got up.

Alana had peed on the last page of Luka's book, which was blank, like all the rest. Luka picked her up, went down to the kitchen, made coffee, fed the dog cornflakes and milk. Alana shat on the sofa and Luka carried her back upstairs because she was just a puppy and couldn't climb up and down on her own. Luka hadn't had heat or electricity for three days. When she called the electrician, his wife answered and started saying how long it had been since she'd seen Luka, she should come by for dessert, but Yannis wasn't there just then, he didn't even come home for lunch these days, he was working on the banker

Dandy's pool—"You know, Luka dear, the one who looks like Elvis Presley, so young, and already a real banker."

"Listen, Kyria Remboukos, I haven't had heat or lights for three days."

"The pool is going to start up on the mountain, Luka, and come all the way down to the last of the olive groves, whole kilometers, it's going to be heated and on a slope, so you step into the shallow part and don't even have to swim, you just slide down and shoot out into the deep end at the bottom, and Yannis is putting the whole thing together, we're talking millions, Luka. Dandy's wife wants to put in plastic jellyfish, too, and maybe even a dogfish or two to give the guests at their parties something to talk about, Mark's going to design them. Luka dear, when are you going to stop by so we can have a drink and catch up?"

Luka slammed down the receiver. She went upstairs and sat down to write, but the phone started ringing, so she grabbed Alana and ran back downstairs. It was the electrician.

"Don't worry, the outage isn't on your end."

"What good does that do me? I'm freezing and I've been living with a candle in my hand!"

"Don't worry, I'm telling you, it's not your fault. I called the electric company, there's something wrong at the plant. They'll have your power back up as soon as the crew gets back from the mountain. I can't say exactly when that'll be, because they went up to the monastery, Kornaros who does the connections is a cantor, and he brought the whole crew up to chant a vigil. It's St. Valentine's Day tomorrow and his assistant Kostas wants to get married and asked Kornaros to chant him wedding hymns, and it only works on the eve of St. Valentine's. He wants to marry Maria, but she wants Yiorgos, who wants Matina. And in their rush to get going the guys flipped some switch by mistake, and now the electricity is out on half the island."

Luka went upstairs again and sat down at her desk. "I have to write." She'd been on the island since summer, now it was February and she hadn't written a word. Each morning she woke up at five, sometimes four, and jumped out of bed longing to write—the book was ready inside of her, every chapter, every sentence, every comma, everything was in its place, perfectly set, and she knew she could do it, since she'd written her first book on the island five years before. But as soon as she sat down at her desk the blank page became a mirror that showed only her own face. "I have to write," she'd say a hundred times, then another hundred, and sometimes on the hundredth she would mess up and have to start all over again from the beginning, and the days passed, the months passed, and the blank page got blanker—"I have to write," Luka said as autumn turned to winter, "I have to write!" she shouted into the empty house, and now it was February and the sea had closed in on her like a ring. As soon as she sat at her desk the book became a reflection, the color green, a round egg, a face peering at her, and she would grab her pen to try and write as fast as she could, but the sentences rose up before her like waves pounding against the pier and the paper drew back, her hand struggled to reach it like a shipwrecked sailor grasping at the rocks of some shore.

Luka remembered the day she had mailed her first book to the States from the post office on the island. It had been February then, too, and she was all alone, and the clerk had said, "Open it so I can see, I don't know what 'manuscript' means." Luka had opened it and looked once more at those sentences that would be traveling so far on their own, sentences this man's dirty, fat hands were now touching, sentences made vulgar by the fact of his reading them, since they took on whatever meaning he gave them as he turned the pages and laughed.

"Really, Luka, I thought you were a serious girl."

"That's what all manuscripts are like."

"Well then, we might as well send it, right?" He spat on the stamps, soaking the envelope with his saliva. When Luka went outside it was raining, all the cafés were closed and she had no one to tell, "I just sent my book to America." She sat down on the wharf next to a fisherman who was mending his nets.

"I just sent my book to America."

"Can you help me thread this needle? I can't see a thing in this damned rain."

"Sure," Luka said, sobbing. "My pleasure."

And now, sitting once more before the same page, with the dog peeing everywhere, with that same chill in the air, and the book inside her splitting and rotting, she pulled Alana onto her lap, unscrewed her pen, tilted her head back, put the pen to her mouth, and drank down every last drop of ink—and the book was lost.

Placido and Ron had made love all night long, not because they felt like it but because they were cold. Placido had the same dream again. He was shaving, and as he lathered his face he felt his father's ghost standing behind him and watching him in the mirror, smiling. Placido didn't dare turn around, or even look in the mirror, but hurriedly wiped off the lather with a towel. Just when he'd finally gotten up the courage to turn around and look, he woke up. He always dreamed this dream at four in the morning, and afterward would lie awake thinking terrible thoughts in Spanish. It was the only time he thought in his native language, he spoke English with Ron, he even dreamed in English, though luckily the ghost in his dream didn't speak because ghosts don't speak—but if it ever did, Placido was sure it would speak in English and that would scare him even more, since his father had only spoken Spanish. *As long as the ghost never says anything, I'll get used to it*, Placido thought. But in the middle of the night this problem of languages seemed insoluble; Placido turned it over in his mind every morning from four to eight as Ron slept by his side, and it frightened him even more than the dream itself. Thousands of times he had imagined his father speaking English, and then one night he dreamed that Ron said something in Spanish, and his father shot back a "Fuck you," and in his terror Placido didn't wake up as he usually did, and the dream kept going until his father called Placido a "filthy faggot," then put on a dress and went to drink tea with some ladies at Princes Gate in London, next door to a Montessori school.

Placido woke at eleven and saw Ron sitting there in his nightshirt, knitting.

"The ghost spoke again," Placido said.

"Spanish?"

"No. English, unfortunately."

"Don't talk to me," Ron said. "I'm planning out the next three years of my life."

"Lots to do?"

"Yes. Don't talk to me. You should get to work, too."

Placido picked up the mask he'd been working on since summer and looked at it. It reminded him of someone, but who? And how could he finish it if he didn't know? He dabbed some red on the cheeks.

Then he stuck a Camel in the mask's mouth. Yes, the man smoked Camels for sure—but who was it?

Maggie had been cooking since morning.

Every day she got up, tucked her three cookbooks under her arm, shut herself up in the kitchen and cooked, listening to Vivaldi. The books were *Elizabethan Cuisine*, *Plato's Symposia*, and *Renaissance Spices and Sauces*. At night they all traveled together with their sense of taste: as they chewed they would become ancient Greeks eating light but complex dishes, would feel like barbarians from the Middle Ages as they tore into bloody meat, or would seem to hear the strains of a mandolin as a scrap of some strange herb stuck in their teeth. Each night was a surprise; they came not for the food, but for the taste of an unfamiliar age— and because only then, around the table, did they finally feel they had arrived somewhere.

Maggie had come to the island to write a bestseller and get rich. But on the first night when she sat down to make an outline, it seemed like so much work that she threw the outline in the fireplace, along with the opening passage: "He asked her to dance a waltz. She looked at him, and passion made her hair stand on end." Something wasn't right, it was more like something out of *King Kong* than a love scene from a bestseller, so the book ended with those very first sentences, on that very first night. Now Maggie cooked all day listening to Vivaldi and had another book in mind, one that was sure to be a hit: *The Earliest Recipes of Homo Sapiens*. She dressed hurriedly, made up her face—she couldn't cook if her face wasn't made up—went into the kitchen, and decided that tonight they would eat Elizabethan.

Mark was the first to arrive. He always came ten minutes early. Each night he swore to himself that he would get there at eight on the dot but he always left early, and no matter how hard he tried to make himself walk slowly, halfway there he would start to run, so he always arrived out of breath. "I wanted to get here before it got dark, I forgot my flashlight again," he would explain, though at this time of year it was dark by four. He would sit by the fire, stick his hands practically into the flames, and ask for some wine. "I quit drinking," he would say to Maggie, though he stank of vodka. "I only drink at night—just social drinking, darling," he would add, as his hands shook.

Ron and Placido arrived at five past eight. Placido was carrying a tray of lemons, each tied with a red bow. "A dessert surprise, Maggie dear, we can open them after dinner."

At a quarter past eight Luka showed up, carrying Alana in a little basket. Stanley and Boris were right behind her. They all sat by the fire, stretching their hands toward the flames. Mark was now sitting a little farther back, gripping his glass. His cigarette had gone out and he held it straight up to keep the ash from falling, staring at Luka's neck, while Luka stared at the flames and thought about Mark. *He's so alone, so innocent, so bad, so pure. He's free, because he has nothing left to lose, that's why he paints the way he does, whereas I can't write a single word, because I love my dog and certain mornings and the tiropitas at the bakery and I'm not ready to die.* Luka could only think when Mark was beside her. Watching the ash on his cigarette grow she would write in her head, and all evening at Maggie's, as Mark lit and stubbed out cigarettes, images, landscapes, bodies rose up before her, her book wrote itself calmly and quietly, stretching out at her feet like a dog, and when she bent to pet it, it opened its tail like a peacock and the thousands of colors became words, sentences, paragraphs, chapters—but as soon as she got home and shut the door, the book would disappear.

"Sometimes you look like a boy," Mark whispered into Luka's ear, laughing. "If you were a boy I'd be in love with you," he continued. No one else had heard. "Maggie dear, a bit more wine, just a drop." Mark lit his thousandth cigarette of the evening. "On nights when I don't come here I go to the bar, and always go home drunk at four in the morning, turn on the tape recorder and talk into it, then fall into bed and listen to my own voice. I can stand anything, except for the silence of four a.m. after the bar. It's not because I'm lonely, I don't feel lonely anymore—I used to, but then I used to feel lots of things—no, it's the silence I can't stand, when the house around me throbs with silence, I become this hole filling up with dirt and rocks, as if debris were falling into me and sticking there, as if I were a house building itself on its own, and I grow stiller and stiller on the inside, petrified, and suddenly, like vertigo, the house falls slowly inward, collapsing into itself inside me, like the crazy woman's house up on the mountain that fell in on itself as if it were crazy too. Last night I came home from the bar so drunk I don't even remember turning on the tape recorder and talking, and when I was in bed and pressed play, my voice surprised me—it was clear, with perfect enunciation, and I was saying, 'I'd like to go to Cheops' Pyramid. To sit precisely in the center, cross-legged, light a cigarette, and spend some time. My house is small, protected. I paint sitting down. My cat is trying to get back at me for not loving her anymore.'"

Mark tossed his cigarette into the fireplace.

"*À table!*" Maggie called. She came out of the kitchen wearing a black velvet cape with a hood, a black mask over her eyes, and black elbow-length gloves. "Elizabethan!" they all cried, clapping their hands. Placido followed carrying a piglet stewed in prunes, stretched on its back in the pan with an orange in its mouth and a bow around its neck.

Maggie curtsied. "Milords, miladies, take a seat!"

Placido turned off the lights, lit the candles, and put on some baroque music. "With your hands!" Maggie ordered, pulling off her gloves.

They all tore off huge chunks, their chins dripped with sauce and blood as their teeth ripped into the meat and their cries of satisfaction mingled with the music. They had learned how to play their roles to perfection, drinking red wine and exchanging silent glances because in Elizabethan times the aristocracy ate without speaking, conversation began only with the fruit course. When they had eaten, Maggie brought out rosewater for them to wash their hands. Ron belched like a Tudor, Boris kissed Stanley, they all said, "Thank you, Lord," and burst out laughing. The game was over. Then came coffee, tea, and flavored cigarettes from the Indies. They moved back in front of the fire.

"Conversation time," Maggie announced.

Ron took out his knitting. He kept his yarn in empty cans of Grandos Café Espresso. The lid of each can matched the color of the yarn inside; tonight it was pink. Ron began to knit incredibly fast, a cigarette dangling from his mouth. "I've been working on this sweater since summer," he said, "and it's all I think about. At night while Placido is dreaming of his father, I quietly get up and knit a row—I didn't know how to bind off the neck and went and asked Kyria Koula for help but she bound it off round and I wanted it square, so I've given up on the neck for now and am doing the peacock on the front, the pink feathers, I brought the green can too in case I have time to start on the tail." Ron smoked and spoke faster and faster as he knitted, and had even started to sweat. Mark put a hand on his shoulder.

"Don't do that. You'll finish your peacock."

"Yes," Ron said and suddenly stopped, tears in his eyes.

"Every time I walk by Sue's house at night I see a bat," Mark said. "It flies slowly over the roof and makes circles in front of the door, always the same bat, every night. One day I saw Sue leaving on the Flying Dolphin, and that night when I passed her house the bat had disappeared. Sue was gone for months and the bat never showed up. Then one day she came back. That night the bat was there again. It struck me as odd."

"Alex told me," Luka said, "that this island is on some secret map of all the places that are supposed to be magical, places that radiate magic or are touched by it. They're connected by a red line that starts in the Carpathians and vanishes somewhere in Asia. And this island is on it."

"Bullshit," Mark said. "Bullshit," he said again, and looked at Luka angrily, because he'd remembered the portrait waiting for him at home, the headless body that watched him as he slept at night.

"What did you all do today?" Maggie always asked exactly at ten.

"I got up at four," Placido said, "finished the mask for the show, took a five-minute break at six, drank some mint tea, then worked on the vase with the Spanish motif until two. That's a total of ten hours of work, and then I made a rice salad for Ron, and at three I lay down and read *The Golden Bough* until eight."

"We stayed in bed all day," Stanley said, gazing tenderly at Boris.

"I wrote nonstop," Luka said. "I threw myself into the second part, I've never worked better, my hand was running all on its own over the page, I've never—"

Mark smiled at her. The sentence hung in the air, unfinished. She flushed and lowered her eyes.

"I've been making plans," Ron said. "Every morning I wake up and make plans. Three-year plans, five-year plans, when I'm really well rested I can even do ten-year plans: where I'll be, who I'll be, what I'll be doing. It's hard work, it's tiring. In the afternoon I take a nap, then make a general plan that incorporates all the other ones. By spring I'll have reached the one hundred and fifty-sixth plan: where I'll be, who I'll be, and what I'll be doing when I'm ninety."

Mark laughed. "I'm not laughing at you, Ron. It's just that you remind me of my ex-wife Beth. She was a drunk, but she was always making plans. Me, the only plan I ever made in my life was to think of her as my ex-wife from the very first time I set eyes on her. Even though we lived together for twenty years."

"I don't find that funny," said Boris.

"Neither do I," answered Mark.

"Then why are you laughing?"

"I don't know."

It was five past eleven, time for Monopoly. They had a special board: the places they bought and sold were all on the island. Luka won Tombazis's house and the post office, Ron lost the bar, Mark lost the bank and two tavernas in Kaminia.

They drank hot chocolate precisely at midnight, then played Victims and Murderers. They drew scraps of paper from a hat. Tonight Mark was the murderer. They turned off the lights and everyone ran to hide. Mark was left alone in the living room, which was illuminated only by the flames in the fireplace. He lit a cigarette. He liked being the murderer. *Maybe in Elizabethan times I'd have been a hangman.* On the nights when he was the murderer, he didn't look for the others right away. Those few minutes when he sat alone by the fire, gathering his strength, clearing his mind, were treasured moments, moments of peace, the only ones he had left. Then he would come to life abruptly as if shedding his skin, as if he'd never drunk a drop in his life, and shout, "Here I come!"—but he would just sit there motionless in the chair, smoking, until his cigarette went out and the moment passed. Then he would rise and climb the stairs, and because he hated the others for stealing those moments from him, he played the murderer to perfection, shouting, "I smell human flesh!" in a voice that made them tremble with fear.

He had reached the upstairs landing. Someone was under the bed, breathing heavily. He sat on the bed, lit a cigarette, bent down and grabbed an arm. It was Luka. They didn't speak. Luka didn't shout for help as she was supposed to. She stayed silent as Mark knelt and stroked the inside of her wrist, then his hand inched higher and gently, tenderly, he put out his cigarette on a vein in her arm that glowed in the dark. The room started to smell like the fireplace downstairs and Mark rested his lips on the wound— he didn't kiss it, just rested his lips on Luka's arm and seemed to forget they were there, so his mouth stayed there for a long time, and Luka closed her eyes and saw her entire book unfolding before her again. It was coming from Mark's mouth, he was whispering it into her wound, and the book entered her bloodstream and rushed through her in a torrent, seeking an exit, begging to be written.

They stayed like that until the others came out of their hiding places. Luka pulled the sleeve of her sweater down over the burn. It was half past one, the time when they always left, so they said goodnight and started down the mountain. At the crossroads they said goodnight again, then went their separate ways.

3

Every afternoon Luka went to give her neighbor
Anezoula a massage. She had recently discovered that
her hands had magical properties—"And since you
can't write, Luka dear," Anezoula had told her three
months before, "why don't you do my leg some
good?" Anezoula adored her, but she was glad that
Luka wasn't writing: she loved her twice as much
when she saw her coming over in tears.

"Did you write anything today?" she would ask.

"No," Luka would answer.

And Anezoula's eyes would shine.

They would go into the parlor where the wood
stove smoked and the TV was always on with the
sound off. Luka would sit on a low stool, Anezoula in
a tall red armchair, thrusting out a foot that reeked of
potatoes and Vaseline and made Luka want to throw
up. Then Anezoula would open her mouth and talk
for hours on end without even pausing for breath.
Outside the sky darkened, but Anezoula never turned
on the light, and the room filled with smoke from the
stove as Luka, half unconscious, listened to Anezoula's
voice coming at her as if from a distance, and the
programs changed on the silent screen.

"… That's how I broke the damned thing, Luka
dear, in Fisher's garden. I was mopping and fell from
four meters up. I know that garden like the back of

my hand, I've been taking care of it for twenty years. That's how I know I didn't fall on my own, and I'm sure it wasn't a human hand that did it. A ghost pushed me from behind, I felt it. Besides, they say ghosts push you around in houses you don't love— and I sure hate Fisher's house! What was I thinking, cursing the patio as I mopped? It heard me, that damned ghost, it was lurking behind the lemon trees. Of course now I can say what I like, the deed's done. Eight thousand miserable drachmas they pay me to take care of four hanging gardens and water all those trees they bring in from Africa that smell like wigs, and when I tell them, in English, 'My leg,' they say, 'Nice legs, Anezoula! Nice legs!' And when I say, 'Insurance card,' they say, 'Nice Greek, Anezoula! Nice Greek!' In summer I see them running naked through the garden, brother and sister hopping around stark naked in the garden I've been watering all winter in my slippers and robe, the two of them ducking behind the lemon trees and the African cactuses, both of them close to seventy and still playing hide-and-seek and who knows what else. Then around August, Mr. Grey's friend Don comes. They put him up in the guest house. The day before he comes I make up the bed with black satin sheets and mop the floor until my hands are about to fall off, all so his pretty little feet won't get dirty. Mr. Don is twenty-five and refuses to wear shoes on the island. 'Anezoula dear,' he says to me in his awful Greek,

'Me island barefoot, because New York only boot.'
'New York only boot,' I say to him, 'but here you show him who's boss.' 'Anezoula, I don't understand,' he says in English. 'To your blindness, then,' I say. At night Mr. Grey goes out into the garden in a gold caftan and hides behind the orange trees. 'Don! Darling! Can I come in?' Then he starts making bird noises, the hoot owl, the screech owl, this year he learned the rooster, too. Tell me, Luka dear, why does he have to squawk like that? Why can't he just go in so the two of them can do it and we can all get some rest instead of being kept up until morning by that racket? 'Maybe they don't ever do it, maybe that's why he shrieks'—that's what Stavros has been saying for years, and it makes me furious. 'Would they be buying him all these plane tickets and jewelry if they didn't do it?' I shout back. 'He's got so much gold on he can hardly walk!' But Stavros just turns on the TV and watches some horror movie until morning, with the volume at full blast so he won't hear the screeching outside. 'Turn off the TV,' I tell him. 'No,' he says, 'it drives me crazy to hear that old faggot pretending he's a hoot owl right out there under my balcony—but I'm telling you, they don't do it.' 'They do it all right, they do it after.' 'After what?' Stavros shouts. 'The old guy's vocal chords are completely shot from all that screeching, he couldn't even drag himself to the kid's bed. They don't do it, I'll put my money on it.' 'Go and ask him!' I shout back. And we

never get a minute's sleep, Luka dear, all summer long. In the morning Miss Cynthia appears in her silk robe with the dragons on it and Matina brings in the silver breakfast tray, sets it down on the table and says, 'Miss Cynthia, do you need me for anything else? If not I'll go and paint.' That's what really gets me: Miss Cynthia owns a gallery, and she's turned our Matina into a painter. She used to graze sheep, now she has shows in Paris, they even put out a book, it's got a black cover with *Matina* written on it in foreign letters. 'Naïve,' that's what Miss Cynthia calls her— must be a pseudonym. And now Matina's back from Paris and comes to see me wearing jeans and with three rings in each ear, she shows me clippings from foreign newspapers with her photograph, and says to me, 'Oh, Anezoula! If only I'd broken my leg too! Then I could paint all day and no one would bother me!' I pretend not to hear and ask, 'Matina dear, how are things?' And she says, '*Ça va.*'"

Luka rubbed Anezoula's leg, went through her exercises. Outside night had fallen and her own house, which she could see from the window, was pitch black, bigger in the dark, and more silent. With each passing day Anezoula talked more and more, faster and faster. When Luka got home at night she couldn't read, or think, or sleep, yet each day she couldn't wait to go to Anezoula's. She was jealous of Anezoula for being able to talk the way she should have been writing: without thinking, without paper, without a pen, with nothing but those wild words, the words Luka herself had lost. And Anezoula knew it. It was as if she were punishing Luka with a better performance each day. Without realizing it, Anezoula had become an artist in order to get back at Luka for having a bigger house, green eyes, and all the men she imagined following Luka around—and so, bit by bit, with the play she put on for Luka each evening, Anezoula had become a master of language.

Kyria Evgenia came by at around eight.

"How are you, Evgenia dear? Have you been working on anyone these days?"

Kyria Evgenia sat down on the sofa. She had no teeth at all and hairs sprouted from her chin.

Luka was afraid of these visits. The atmosphere changed; Anezoula lowered her voice, became tender with her.

"There was a full moon," Kyria Evgenia said. "I worked on her for three days and nights. She'll get him for sure, now that he drank the beer. We mixed him up for good. For three days and nights I said the words at the crossroads—and if he doesn't take her now, he'll fall down just as he is and won't be able to drink so much as a glass of water."

"And our Luka here, when will we marry her off?" Anezoula asked. "Luka dear, don't shake your head, deep down it's what you want—don't I always know what you want?"

"Yes," Luka answered softly, "you always know."

"At least tell her the words, so she'll know them, and later we can do the real work," Kyria Evgenia said.

"When a girl is in love," Anezoula began, "but for some reason she can't get married and has wandered the world without success, suddenly a close friend of hers will appear and say, 'I can help you with the situation that's been tormenting you.' On this island there's a magic mirror that an old woman has been working with for forty years. First, the mirror dissolves any ties the girl might have, so she can get married. The girl doesn't even need to be there, she just sends her request by way of some friend and right away, if it's a tough case, the old woman passes the young man who's refusing the marriage through the mirror, and after he's been spun around three times he stands still, and she asks him, 'Which do you choose, the girl or the curse?' As soon as he answers she begins her work, the curse takes hold and burns, the girl is released, the boy says yes, and they come together. If the situation is even tougher, she pulls a ribbon. After the first meeting, in order for the marriage to take place, the young man has to drink a beer that's also been worked on and passed through the mirror. The moment he drinks it he starts to fall in love with her, and then he has to drink another beer that's been passed through the mirror three times. Then he starts to feel dizzy, people talk to him and he doesn't answer, he just thinks."

It was ten o'clock. Kyria Evgenia left, Stavros

came home and turned on the TV, the massage was over, Anezoula finally stopped talking. Luka said goodnight. When she got home she drank two bottles of black ink, each in a single swallow. Now all she had left was red, and she never wrote in red.

4

"Pass."

"Ten thousand."

"I'll stay."

"Fold," said Mark.

Freddy dealt the second card face-up. "Ace bets," he said.

"Fifty thousand," said Alex.

"Either you have a pair of aces or you're bluffing."

"I'm in at fifty," Freddy said.

"Me too," said Klaus.

The third card was dealt face-down.

"A hundred thousand," said Alex.

"In," said Freddy.

"Five hundred thousand," said Klaus.

"You're bluffing. I'll see you," said Alex.

Freddy bit his cigar.

"Me too," he said, "and I'm dealing the fourth face-up. I bet first, pair of kings. Eight hundred thousand."

"I'll see you," said Alex.

The game unfolded with such speed and precision that their eyes glazed over with concentration. Mark and Klaus were both out; the only ones left were Alex and Freddy, who dealt the last card face-down.

"A million," Alex said.

"A million and a half, everything I've got with me, and a check for the rest." Freddy signed with a

Montblanc and tossed the check onto the table.

"Two million," Alex said. "The banks are closed, but I'll call Geneva in the morning, you'll have the money by afternoon."

"I'm in, I want to see your hand." Freddy grabbed the Montblanc again and signed a second check.

"What've you got?" he asked.

Alex spread out his cards.

"Full house, aces and queens. Couldn't you tell I had the aces from the beginning? I'm in no rush for the money, wire it to my account in Geneva."

Freddy showed his own hand.

"Royal flush. Didn't you know I wouldn't have stayed in if I didn't have the hand? I'm in no rush for the money, just put it in my account in Zurich."

Alex had gone bright red and was having trouble breathing. Freddy laughed, took out a cigarette, lit it, and put it in Alex's mouth.

"Come on, Kopesky, pull yourself together. You'll win it all back next Saturday. You always play so aggressively, Alex, that you forget to think about anyone else's game. You're always talking about the cool you need in poker, but when the game gets going, you play like a nymphomaniac. Remember what we were saying about female frigidity, how exciting it is, and how it's just like the cool in poker?"

Alex laughed. "Remember Christina? We had her between us, a fire blazing in the fireplace and Ravel's *Bolero* playing so loud you could hear it all the way down at the harbor, and she just lay there counting the beams on the ceiling. We did everything for her, and in the morning she said, 'There are four hundred, and the ones on the far right are all worm-eaten.'"

"These days I only sleep with frigid women," Freddy said, "as practice for poker. And poker teaches me new techniques, new caresses, so complex that even the most frigid women melt at my touch—but all those bodies opening themselves up to me are just boring, while poker resists all caresses, it always keeps its cool. It only gives in to me when I win, and I to it when I lose."

"*C'est ça l'amour*," said Klaus, who had lost two houses in London that night.

The game was over. Alex tallied up everyone's debts.

"Mark, you owe eight hundred thousand. Do you want to pay in paintings or cash?"

"Paintings."

"Have you done them yet?"

"No."

"I want mine by four o'clock Saturday."

"Landscapes or nudes?"

"Why bother asking, since all you ever paint are headless boys?"

"I want a nude of that kid who sings at church." Freddy said. "Make the hips sort of feminine, and paint a royal flush around his belly button." Then he added, "Don't bother doing the head," and everyone laughed. But they all collected Mark's paintings and guarded them carefully—they knew that one day they'd be worth millions, and when they had no money left to bet with, they played for paintings. And the paintings went from one house to another as Alex won, or Klaus; after each game the mule would come to carry the paintings from one hillside to the next. On Saturdays when they played at Freddy's or Alex's the paintings would be hanging on the walls, but Klaus kept his in storage for safety. The only one who didn't own a single one of his paintings was Mark.

The game was over. They had been playing for two days. It was five a.m. on the seventeenth of February, and Mark, as always, had lost. These days he only painted so he could play poker, and he worked so hurriedly, to finish in time for the next game, that all his paintings seemed unfinished: boys lying on sofas with sketched-in hands, half-eaten faces, gestures that seemed to go nowhere, and landscapes in the background that were barely penciled in. Thus his haste led to an exquisite abstraction, and in order to play poker each Saturday, Mark was creating masterpieces. He had no idea, but the others knew and didn't say anything, as the paintings piled up in their storerooms, waiting.

At night as Mark painted, each face, each leg, would become an ace, a queen, a flush, a full house. As he stood there drunk under the spotlight, the rest of the house sunk in darkness, his hand never shook, the precision of his movements was absolute—and it was strange, because he drank constantly; as soon as he put down his brush he would start trembling so much that he'd have to sit down and clench his teeth to keep them from chattering, clasp his hands behind his back to keep himself from scratching at his face. On these nights, with each stroke of the brush he would whisper: "This red will bring me a full house, this black a flush; I won't do the mouth so Freddy will lose; I'll leave the leg only half finished so Klaus will fold; maybe I'll beat Alex with a flush if I leave off the head."

The game was over.

It was February, and it was raining. They all lit cigars. It was time for their story: the winner always told.

"I'm going to tell you about Leonora," Freddy said, then got up, lit the candles, and switched off the lights. "I remember the first time I saw Leonora, here on the island, I felt as if I knew her from somewhere, as if we'd passed each other on the street as children on our way to school, as if I'd seen her often in my sleep. So when I saw her here, I wasn't really surprised. The same thing has happened to me with lots of people I've met on the island: they seem familiar, as if I met them once, briefly, as a child, and back then, with a single glance, we made a secret plan to meet here years later for some reason that was both particular and unknown. I felt the same way about you guys. So when I saw Leonora sitting at the bar one night drinking a tequila sunrise, I went and sat next to her and we drank all night, not talking, just listening to George playing "My Way" on the piano. Leonora was thin and always wore white. She had a long face with something unfinished about it, like Mark's paintings, only her eyes were small and clever, like the eyes on dolls, or sharks. There was something romantic about her, but something vulgar, too. I can't really describe her any better than that, because the thing is, she was crazy, and always borrowed from the gazes of others in order to exist—she didn't have anything that was permanently hers, truly her own, since each gaze showed her in a different light, as a different person. Each time I saw her she was some other Leonora who belonged to the gaze of whoever had seen her last—I was just looking at leftovers, fragments, the disjointed pieces others had left.

"Leonora was an alcoholic. At night when the bar closed we'd find her passed out in the trash, cats eating fish heads off her white clothes. But we always left her there, she liked it, she got really mad whenever we carried her home. At six the next morning she would wake up, put on some lipstick, and go to Antonio's for coffee.

"Before she came here she had been Batista's mistress for years. 'In Cuba, darling,' she'd say. One night at the bar she told me the whole story: 'Freddy dear, I was crazy about him. He was ugly and bald, but no one had ever made love to me like that. And of course he was a dictator, too, which I found very exciting. I was his official mistress, I lived in the palace and ruled Cuba along with him. I threw huge parties with fireworks, I organized picnics for the officers' wives, exquisite banquets for the ministers, field days at the schools. I was the only one who was allowed to go into Batista's office when he was giving orders for torture and executions. I would turn the pages of names and he would read off the lists of people to be arrested into the phone and, darling, the names were so beautiful, it was as if I were turning the pages of a score by Bach! We always made love afterward, it turned me on to think that at that exact moment all those beautiful names were being tortured.'" Freddy laughed. "That was Leonora. She told me the whole story at the bar, drinking cocktails, as if she were chatting about the latest fashions, or whispering about some man sitting next to us whom she found 'gorgeous.' With Leonora everything was always 'gorgeous'—the man sitting beside her, the torture cells, Cuba, this island, the piles of trash awaiting her at night. When Batista lost Cuba, he lost Leonora too. When the guerillas stormed into the palace and set it on fire, for a minute Leonora thought about joining those gorgeous revolutionaries, but when she heard them shouting, 'Batista, we want your whore!' she thought better of it and told him, 'Darling, if you don't give me five million dollars right now, in cash, I'll throw all the top-secret files off the balcony.' A short while later, Leonora appeared on the island. She bought a villa and went from being the First Lady of Cuba to the first lady of the island. But the island had no executions or beautiful names, and pretty soon Leonora got bored and became an alcoholic. Her new craze was Americans—'They really know how to drink, darling.' And instead of executions, she invented a new game that excited her just as much: every night she would choose a new man—an American—and they would take the Flying Dolphin back to the mainland, go to the airport with no baggage, no money, just their credit cards, and get on whatever plane happened to be leaving next. So they'd end up in Alaska one day, Moscow or Tahiti the next. They never left the airport, they just went to the bar and drank themselves blind—vodka in Russia, punch in the Seychelles, tequila in Mexico—then came straight back home. That night at Bill's, Leonora would teach us the Eskimo word for 'screwdriver,' and we'd all die laughing. The next day she'd pick someone else.

"But one day Leonora fell in love. His name was David, he was a twenty-year-old English kid who drank nothing but orange juice. So Leonora quit drinking too. David would lie in bed all day reading *For Whom the Bell Tolls*. 'Hemingway has action,' he'd say, 'that's why I like him.' He made love as if writing a book that was missing its central idea. Months passed. One day Leonora started having dizzy spells. She went to the doctor and was told she only had one year to live. She found it very romantic. David started reading *The Magic Mountain*. Leonora sold the house, put on a white veil and took David to Deauville, where they got a suite in a hotel by the sea. Leonora sent me a postcard of the beach that read, *Darling, I want to die in style. Kisses, L.* In the afternoons they walked on the deserted beach, all in white, carrying a white umbrella under the white rain beside the white waves. Leonora was beautiful in the role of the dying woman, with her fur and her long, narrow face, her clever eyes. They ate caviar and drank champagne, and David became an alcoholic, too. And since he was drunk all the time, he soon fell madly in love with her, shut up all day in that room with the champagne and the caviar and the idea of death. But when the year was up, Leonora still hadn't died. Her cheeks had taken on a rosy glow, she'd even gained a few pounds. Then one morning David died of alcohol poisoning. Leonora found herself alone, alive, and broke, since she'd budgeted her money to last just a year. She was furious with the doctor who had made the mistake. She sold her fur and went to live in a tiny village in Portugal where all her lovers were fishermen, and instead of champagne and caviar she drank barreled brandy and ate sardines. Another year passed and she still hadn't died. Around that time I lost track of her. Then last summer I ran into Finley at the bar, he said he'd heard news of Leonora from some guy he'd met at a bar on the Portuguese border. Leonora had become a nun, and a saint, too. The story has it that one night while she was sleeping, drunk, in the village trash, she was visited by Christ. A wild, angry Christ who wore jeans and carried a knife. Leonora insisted he was smoking Players, too, to make her think of the word 'prayers.' He pointed to a nunnery up on the mountain, ground out his cigarette with his boot, and disappeared. When the *mère supérieure* opened the door, Leonora, covered in fish bones, shouted, 'I saw Him!' The door closed behind her, and a year later her statue was in all the churches in Portugal. And that's the story of Leonora."

Everyone was silent. Freddy, sweating, asked for some brandy.

The game was over. It was February, and raining, and soon they would have to head back to their empty houses, to walk through the dark, empty streets, crawl into their damp beds, and fend off their dreams. Each one prayed in his own way for something to happen. None of them noticed that the texture of the night had changed, that the sky was breathing like skin, throbbing and winding itself around the island like a spider's web.

5

Luka was sitting at her desk.

"I'm dying," said Kyria Angeliki next door. Luka's window opened onto her yard. Kyria Angeliki had been dying all winter. She sat out in the yard from morning on, and all day long she looked at the sea and said, "I'm dying." She had come down from the mountain to die at her son's house, but her daughter-in-law, Kyria Theodora, hated her. She made her sit outside when it was cloudy and as soon as the sun came out she would pick her up, chair and all, and shut her up in the kitchen. Angeliki would stretch her hand toward the sun, eyes welling with tears, and say, "Light." "It's not good for you," Theodora would snap.

Visiting hours were in the late afternoon.

"I'm dying," Angeliki would say.

"We know, Angeliki dear, we know," the women from the neighborhood said, eating marzipan. They sat in a ring around her, and each day the circle of chairs drew closer and closer until Angeliki was barely visible in the center. At night she sat alone on the terrace, looking up at the sky and saying, "Stars." She was calm and happy, waiting for death as if it were some sweet, pleasant event, as if it were simply a visit she was going to pay someone she loved and missed. Luka loved her, though they had never spoken. All winter long she had been secretly following Angeliki's daily walk toward death, watching her through half-closed shutters, and each day Angeliki got smaller and smaller, more and more like a baby.

Luka went over to Anezoula's. It was raining, the parlor was dark, the TV on with no sound. "Rub my leg," Anezoula said. "Today I'm going to tell you about the unbaptized baby, so turn off the TV and light the candle. The baby was mine."

Luka tenderly touched the swollen leg, looking at the veins and broken bones.

"Maybe I should leave?"

"No," Anezoula said harshly. "If I don't tell you, who will I tell? It happened twenty-five years ago today, on the eighteenth of February. It all happened in a single night, so fast that the next morning I thought it had been dream. The pains came on at seven that evening and I gave birth right away, within twenty minutes, to a baby boy. All the women from the neighborhood came with flowers and sweets, Stavros danced one *zeimbekiko* after another, back then his mother was living with us, too, and she made coffee for the guests all night long in the kitchen, singing, as I gazed at the baby and thought, 'I have a son.' Around dawn it got very cold and my mother-in-law took the baby from me and said, 'It's freezing, I'll bring him downstairs where it's warm.' She lit a fire in the coal stove and pushed the crib up next to it, and an hour later the baby was dead from the fumes. The women cried and pulled at their hair, cursing my mother-in-law to the same kind of death, then the doctor came, looked at the baby, and said, 'I'd have to be Christ himself to save this child.' And I started to scream, 'He's not baptized! Not one of you thought to pick him up and baptize him in air before he died so my baby could go to his grave with a name!' Then everyone kneeled, held hands, and prayed:

> I believe in one God
> Omnipotent Father
> Creator of Heaven and Earth
> And all things seen and unseen…

While they were praying, Stavros put the dead baby on a silver tray—that's what you did in those days when the baby hadn't been baptized—and went to the graveyard alone, to bury it without a priest, to dig a grave with his own shovel and bury his child. I'll never forget the look on his face as he walked past by my bed and turned to me and said, 'Anezoula, tell me, in God's name, what kind of father can bear to bury his child alone, to throw it into the ground like a dog?' I was going to call the baby Manolis."

That night Luka dreamed that a blond man was standing with his back to her so she couldn't see his face. He was sad and kept saying, "My name is Manolis," and Luka cried and shouted, "You don't have a name, you're not baptized!" Then he started to turn his head and Luka was gripped by such an overwhelming sense of dread, she didn't want to see his face, she knew she shouldn't, but he kept turning, now she could see one of his cheeks—"No!" Her own voice woke her. The house was still, silent. "No!" she shouted. "No! No! No!"

She drank a glass of milk in the kitchen. "No," she said again, but this time quietly, absentmindedly, watching the rain hit against the windowpanes.

It was the beginning of March but the days were dark, it rained constantly and instead of spring coming, winter strengthened its hold. Luka still went to Anezoula's every day, but she didn't go to Maggie's anymore, or down to the harbor; she had even stopped answering the phone. All day she sat motionless at her desk, then at six she got up, put on her galoshes and went to Anezoula's; the only things left were Anezoula and her broken leg, the dark room, the silent screen.

And the stories.

"Luka dear, yesterday you left five minutes early, so today we'll go until eight twenty, and I'll tell you the story of the little pig."

"Sure," Luka said, smoothing Vaseline onto Anezoula's leg. The smell didn't bother her anymore. Anezoula smiled, the performance began.

"Once upon a time there were three young

sisters. Someone cast a spell on them out of spite, and one day as they were coming home they slipped and fell in front of their door. Two of the three took to their beds, and the one who was hurt the least badly took care of them. One night she heard terrible cries coming from the room her sisters shared and she ran to see what was wrong. They were both sitting up in bed, one bleating like a sheep, the other mooing like a cow. The girl cried for help, all the neighbors came running, but no one could get close to the sisters. They finally managed to tie them down, then the priest came to try to exorcize the spirits, but nothing worked. They stayed in bed for four years, without food, without water, and all day and night one would bark like a dog while the other bleated like a sheep, then one would meow like a cat while the other played the donkey. Everyone was too scared to go near them, until one day a woman brought over some greens and milk from her house. She tossed the greens to the one who was bleating and gave the milk to the one who was mewing, and the girls threw themselves on the food, tearing each other's night-gowns in their hunger. They've been living like that ever since, possessed, tied to their beds—by now they're old women and a little girl comes and throws some hay and a bottle of milk through the window, no one has set foot in the house for fifteen years. Luka, we still have another fifteen minutes, you always start rushing toward the end, I can feel it in your hands. Do you want me to tell you the story of the little pig?"

"Anezoula, I'm tired, I can't listen to any more stories."

"Of course you can. Once there was a couple, the husband was a sailor, the wife a seamstress. He went off on a voyage and left his wife alone with their child, who was two years old. One night a shade passed over the woman while she was sleeping, and when the child woke up it started squealing like a pig. The mother went crazy. She fell into bed with the child, shouting, 'Quick, take this bar of soap away!' Of course there was no soap to be seen. Then she said, 'Quick, take this pig and butcher it!' And she started to hit her child, and beat it to death. A few hours later she died, too. Her husband happened to return from his voyage the very day of the funeral, and joined the funeral march without knowing that his own wife and child were in the coffins. At the cemetery, when he saw the names on the graves, he took out his revolver and shot himself."

Luka left at a run. That night she dreamed that a huge pig was sitting on the edge of her bed, watching her. "What's your name?" she asked.

And it laughed and said, "Why are you asking, when you already know?"

6

It was the day of the Carnival parade.

All of the masqueraders were men in drag. They had been gathering since morning, and by noon the harbor was packed.

First came the construction workers, dressed as schoolgirls with hair ribbons, blue frocks with white collars, hairy legs, and heavy work boots. They carried red schoolbags and their nails were black with cement.

Behind them were the whores, with fake breasts, fake eyelashes, fishnet stockings and skirts slit to mid-thigh, wigs, red lipstick, high heels that kept getting stuck between the paving stones. They were all smoking Marlboros, and when the cigarette touched their lips they would inhale with exaggerated femininity, then dab their lips with a tissue to keep their lipstick perfect.

Behind them was Yannis the electrician, alone in the middle of the line, dressed as a widow. He was wearing one of his grandmother's black dresses and a veil he'd affixed with a wall socket, and he'd colored his eyelids, eyebrows, and lips with magic marker. Then came Kostas the plumber, dressed as a ghost in a white miniskirt, boots, and gloves, a white plastic bag on his head with two holes cut in it for his eyes.

At noon the bride who would be leading the parade arrived, wearing a white wedding dress smothered in lace, her face hidden behind a mask with a black skull on it. The train on her veil was at least three meters long, and a mule dressed as a house in a huge cardboard box with painted windows and doors held the end in its teeth. The drums and tabors began to play, everyone got in line, and the parade started off. They passed by the waterfront cafés dancing the *tsiftiteli*, blowing kisses and showing their legs, then headed toward the bakery.

"Bravo, boys! To the most handsome men on the island!" the baker's wife Archonto cried as she smashed a bottle of whiskey on the pavement at their feet.

Maggie, Alan, Placido, and Ron were sitting at the third café. Alan was very pale and wore his long black Burberry raincoat, as always. He had brought a bottle of Martell and a box of After Eight mints with him, and was telling them about some young Australian writer who had written a book without a single word it in, just periods and exclamation points. "Words are meaningless," Alan was saying, "it's the feeling that counts—that's what I'm trying to get across in my book, too."

"So did you end up buying part of the bar?" Placido asked.

"Yes, it'll be an experience, I took Stephanos's half, so now I'm stuck here again. Last year I had finally decided to leave, but then I met Adelina, who wouldn't let me out of bed for a year, and this year Bill won't let me out of the bar...."

"So when do you find time to write?" Maggie asked.

Just then the Carnival parade arrived. As soon as Placido saw them he licked his lips and said, "*Oh là là!*" The masqueraders started dancing around their table. Ron bent and whispered something to Alan, they burst out laughing, and Alan said to Maggie, loud enough for people at the neighboring tables to hear, "Look at the fags!"

Everyone in the café started laughing, and some American shouted, "It kills me, man!"

Then one of the whores, a carpenter named Thodoris who spoke English, went over to Alan, put out his cigarette in the glass of cognac Alan was raising to his lips, and began to gyrate in front of him, until his stomach was practically touching Alan's nose. No one was laughing anymore.

"We dress as whores once a year, for fun," Thodoris said. "You, you'll be faggots your whole life. When I was working on your house in those jeans you liked, you were always coming in to see what I was doing, you wouldn't let me work, you kept asking, Thodoris, what color should we paint the bathroom, Thodoris, how about a dark pink, with just a touch of purple, Thodoris, would you like some Brazilian coffee, Thodoris, stay a while after the others have left, Thodoris, is that a new belt you're wearing?'"

The masqueraders, who had formed a ring around the table, started to sing:

Thodoris, what color should we do the bathroom,
    Aman! Aman!
A dark pink, with just a touch of purple,
    Aman! Aman!

The crowd of onlookers clapped and sang along. Placido watched them uneasily and said "*Oh là là*" again. Then Thodoris abruptly peeled his stomach away from Alan's face and shouted, "Let's go, guys!"

The parade turned and disappeared down a narrow side street, the crowd following behind. The only ones left on the waterfront were the foreigners. Suddenly a breeze came up and the sky clouded over—and though it was early afternoon, the darkness was absolute.

In the narrow streets the drums grew louder, the sky went blacker, the fishnet stockings gleamed like steel, wigs flapped in the breeze like metal wings. Through some window a radio announced that a storm watch was in effect, then started playing rock music. The paraders reached their first stop outside Kyria Theoni's market. The neighbors had filled the square with tables covered with carafes of wine. The masqueraders started to drink, and kept drinking as the neighbors brought out more wine, and when they'd drunk all there was they got up to dance. The whores were dancing the *tsiftiteli* in pairs, one kneeled and leaned her head back while the other danced in circles around her and poured wine into her mouth. One of the whores gyrated so fast that her garter snapped and she said "Dammit" in a deep voice and asked for a cigarette.

The schoolgirls gathered under the window where the radio was, dancing to the rock music. Their hairy legs flew through the air, the bows in their hair twisted around and dangled in front of their noses, some did fancy moves that made their underwear show. The crowd stomped their feet to the rhythm as someone said, "Come on, mama, give it all up," and someone else shouted, "Give it to me, baby."

Suddenly the mule that was dressed as a house, having drunk an entire carafe of wine, went wild. It burst into the market and ate all the halva Kyria Theoni had put on display at the front of the store. Kyria Theoni tried to catch it but it kicked her, she fell on her back, and the cardboard house fell on top of her. She stuck her head out the window and screamed.

The mule bolted outside again, and the bride lunged, mounted it, and stood up on its back, tore off her gown so that all she was wearing was her jeans, her blue galoshes, and the three-meter veil, then sat down and spurred the animal on, shouting, "Whoever catches me is the groom!"

The mule started to run, the bride's veil fluttering in the air as everyone tried to catch it. When she got to the big flight of stairs leading down to the sea, the bride hunched over the mule's back, buried her face in its mane, and disappeared. The mule ran so fast that the veil seemed to be descending the stairs all on its own. Its hoofbeats echoed as if thousands of mules were charging down the mountain. By the time they reached the taverna on the waterfront the mule was frothing, and the bride used her veil to wipe away the sweat dripping from the animal's rump.

The storm broke suddenly. Huge waves rose up, the wind knocked the glasses from the tables, rain fell into the wine.

"Yannis! Yannis!" shouted Nikos, the taverna owner. "Where is he, guys? How am I supposed to recognize him in all these frills? I need Yannis the electrician—come on, guys, show me which one's him or I'm screwed!"

A schoolgirl pointed at the widow.

"That's him."

Nikos ran over and grabbed him by the skirt.

"Yannis, it's all over for me! Something's wrong with the walk-in fridge where I keep the meat, it'll rot on me. Please just take a look, I'm begging you, Yannis, there are two hundred chickens hanging in there!"

"Okay."

"Do you have your tools?"

Yannis lifted his skirt. There was a little bag hanging from his belt.

"Never leave home without it. Like a doctor."

"Flashlight?"

Yannis pulled something from his pocket that looked like a cigarette.

"Videstar. Latest model. Electronic."

"Come on, then. Let's go."

They ran into the taverna. Nikos opened the door of the fridge, they leaned a ladder against the wall, and Yannis climbed up with the flashlight while Nikos held his dress.

"The safeties need changing. Hand me the screwdriver. And three 300-watt fuses. I hope you've got a good hold on that ladder, I've got no balance in these heels."

"You'd think we were in the operating room," Nikos muttered.

"That's how we professionals are," Yannis replied. "Fridge, operating room, it's all the same." A moment later the lights came back on, the compressor started whirring, the whole walk-in fridge started to tremble and hum. Yannis went to climb down, but one of his heels got stuck on a rung of the ladder. He yanked his foot and the ladder started to sway, and to keep it from falling, Nikos let go of the dress, its hem brushed the floor, Nikos stepped on it and ripped off the whole skirt, so Yannis was left standing there in just the bodice and his underwear. He watched as the dress fell slowly to the floor like a parachute, tears of rage springing to his eyes.

"Get your foot off my dress, you idiot! Look what you've done, you've ruined me—it's my grand-mother's dress and she'll kill me, it's taffeta, and she warned me, she said, 'Yannis, if you don't bring that dress back exactly as I gave it to you you'll be sorry, I'll cut you out of my will, I'll take away all the TVs and refrigerators and ovens and you'll have to go and sell worry beads to the tourists.' Lord help me, what am I going to do? Why'd you have to go and blow a fuse today, Nikos? Couldn't it have waited until tomorrow?"

"Are you crazy, Yannis?" Nikos shouted up at him. "It's your fault for wearing those heels!"

"That's the thanks I get for changing your fuses on a holiday?"

Yannis had started to sweat. The black marker on his face had melted and was running down his face, particularly from the eyebrows, which had come together to form a huge bow over his eyes, giving him a surprised expression. Nikos looked at him, hanging from the ladder in his embroidered bodice, underwear, and heels, and burst out laughing, pointing at Yannis and laughing so hard he could hardly speak.

"Do you have any idea what you look like, man? Yannis, have you taken a good look at yourself? Really, you know what you look like? You look just like the Queen of Sheba in that movie we saw with Heracles—sorry, don't take it the wrong way, I can't help it, I'll die of laughter, I'll die and you'll have to carry me over to the cemetery in your heels."

Nikos suddenly let go of the ladder, sat down on the floor, and clenched his stomach with both hands, tears of laughter streaming from his eyes. The ladder toppled to the right and Yannis found himself in midair. He grasped at two rabbits hanging from hooks, then fell flat on his face on the floor. The two men started fighting. Yannis kicked at Nikos with his heels, Nikos grabbed a chicken and hit Yannis over the head with it. "I'll tear this place apart! There won't be a wire left in the whole place!" Yannis shouted as they got tangled up in the dress, hitting at one another blindly. "I'll shove a converter up your ass!" Yannis howled as chickens and rabbits fell from the hooks into the tangle of taffeta. Hearing the commotion, the masqueraders ran to the door of the walk-in fridge and started shouting and placing bets. "Give it to him, Yannis! Make his lights spin!"

"No, his fuses!"

"Come on, widow! Come on, Yannakis!"

The thousand-drachma notes fell like rain, spun through the air, stuck to the hanging chickens, to the rabbits on the floor, to the walls, to Yannis's bare thighs. The crowd howled and pushed to get through the door; someone fainted.

"Beat it, guys! It's the police!"

They all ran back outside, the musicians playing loudly to cover the sound of their footsteps. Yannis and Nikos hurriedly hung the poultry back on the hooks and ran to catch up with the others.

It was raining hard, and at the bend in the road they slowed down. The bride on the mule was going slowly now, smoking. The schoolgirls were smoking, too, and talking shop; their feet had taken on the heavy step of their working days.

"How much do you get at Dandy's?"

"Eight thousand a day, but he works us to the bone. He bought up half the mountain and has no idea what he wants to do with it. One day he tells us to build, that night he screws his wife and the next day he tells us to tear it all down. His wife wanted twenty water jets in her Jacuzzi so the water would hit her from all sides. What a woman, I'd like to hit her from all sides, she'd heat up like an oven. Her husband must not screw her that well, that's why she needs all those Niagaras. What do you say, guys, does that sound about right?"

The schoolgirls walked on, hands in their pockets, and behind them the whores, two by two, smoking constantly, offering one another cigarettes, tossing the empty packs to the side of the road, pulling lighters from their pockets that wouldn't light in the rain, so they had to light each cigarette from another. The rain had washed the makeup from their faces, revealing their eyes, noses, and mustaches. They took off their wigs and threw them onto the street. They didn't look like masqueraders anymore, but like laborers headed home covered in mud.

They came to the last taverna. It was closed. The tables were stacked beneath a plastic sheet that was flapping in the wind. On a chair in the middle of the patio sat Mark, alone on a chair. He was soaked to the skin, holding a drenched cigarette. He kept trying to raise it to his mouth but his hands were shaking, and his legs and head, even his teeth were chattering. Everyone stopped and stared. One little kid shouted, "Mom! Look at him dance!"

Then a boy with black curls broke loose from the crowd, ran over to Mark and offered him a paper rose. Mark took it and started to chew the petals. The boy watched Mark's mouth as if hypnotized, inching closer and closer.

"Now eat the stem, I bet you can't."

Mark chewed the stem and swallowed it. It was full of wires. He looked the boy in the eye and the boy suddenly dropped to his knees, gazing up at him in awe, then bent his head and rested it on Mark's lap. Mark reached out a hand and stroked the rain-drenched curls, saying, "It doesn't matter." The boy leaned his cheek against Mark's knee as if thanking him for having eaten the flower. "It doesn't matter," Mark said again as his tears mingled with the rain. "Salome…" he whispered. Then he sunk his fingers deep in the child's curls, leaned his head back, looked up at the sky, and shouted, "It doesn't matter!"

No one could stop the schoolgirl who ran at Mark, howling and brandishing a knife in the air. She grabbed him by the hair, pulled his head even farther back, and pressed the blade to his neck. For a moment all three of them stayed like that, frozen.

Then the schoolgirl started to speak, looking out at the crowd, and the crowd watched as if a play were unfolding before them—a few people even sat down cross-legged in the rain.

"That's my kid there, you know. That's my boy you're trying to seduce. What did my kid ever do to you, you old faggot? He's my kid, my son, he's in first grade, and you had to choose him? You touched my son with your filthy hands—you'll pay for it, you hear? He's in first grade and I pay for him to learn violin, my son takes violin lessons and you touched him. I work on construction sites to raise him, I spit blood, you bastard, so my son can play the violin, and you pet his hair and cast a spell on him—he doesn't even fall like that at his own mother's knees. All you foreigners can go screw one another in your Londons and your Australias, but leave our kids alone, you hear?"

Mark was shaking all over; no one could tell whether he was laughing or crying, and when the schoolgirl saw, she wiped the lipstick from her mouth with the back of her hand, spit in Mark's face, and withdrew the knife from his neck. "It doesn't matter," Mark said again, looking at him. And the schoolgirl saw such relief and gratitude in his eyes, such impatience, that she stood for a minute with the knife in the air. Then someone grabbed her from behind and snatched the knife away.

"Who is it?" the schoolgirl shouted.

"The keeper of order."

She turned and saw the uniform. Manolis was smiling, but he had a tight hold on her arm.

"Pity it started to rain, it ruined your parade."

"Yes, officer."

"I didn't know your son played the violin, I'll have to come and hear him sometime."

"Yes, officer."

"Now get going. I'll take care of the rest, it's my job."

The schoolgirl took her son by the hand and led him away. They slowly climbed the stairs leading away from the harbor, the schoolgirl's hand resting on the child's curls. The parade and the crowd followed behind, everyone climbing in silence until they disappeared around the bend.

They were alone, Mark in the chair, Manolis standing. Mark looked at him and realized that the headless figure waiting for him on his easel was Manolis. He wondered how he hadn't realized before. For so long he had been running into him at the station, on the street, at the cafés, and had never seen it. He hadn't even noticed how surprisingly handsome Manolis was, with his green eyes, his blond hair, and that glow. *Maybe it's the rain*, he thought. *Yes, it must be the rain, it always lends a face that fleeting radiance. Maybe even the kid with the rain-soaked curls, if I were to see him playing his violin in the kitchen with his mother frying fish at the stove, I might think he was hideous. Then again, it's my job to study faces—so how could such a face, such a gaze have escaped me?* Then, studying Manolis more carefully, Mark felt something else: he had noticed this face from the beginning, but had forgotten on purpose, because only now had the time come for this face to exist. Why that might be the case, Mark neither knew nor cared.

Manolis lit a cigarette, and as he raised his hand to his mouth, Mark finally saw before him the finished portrait, the cigarette finally approaching a face: Manolis's face. And he felt as if he were being wrapped not just in the rain but in the sweet scent of death, because with the portrait's completion it was as if the earth were entering a new orbit—and again, he didn't know why, and didn't care. He realized that now he would paint again the way he had painted as a child, unhurried and carefree. He got up to leave. When they reached the side of the road the two men looked at one another once more, then Mark climbed the stairs while Manolis took the path by the sea.

That night they found Alex Kopesky's body. He had been thrown to the water's edge from a great height. His back was lodged on a rock that had driven itself almost all the way through his chest. The authorities decided it must have been murder; there was no way he could have fallen so precisely on the tip of that particular rock. The old woman who found him kept saying how what struck her most was the smile on the corpse's face as it gazed up at the sky.

7

The day after Kopesky died, Mark finished the portrait. It was Manolis, and once again Mark wondered how for so long he hadn't realized who he was painting. It was Manolis, and Mark painted the head as he had seen it the day before in the rain, with Manolis's blond hair stuck to his face, raindrops coursing down his cheeks. The effect was strange, since the body, completely dry, seemed to belong to someone else.

Manolis's green eyes followed him everywhere from the easel. Once, absentminded, Mark started to light the cigarette Manolis was lifting to his mouth. From a certain corner of the room the portrait reminded him of Luka, and that bothered him. He had never noticed a resemblance, but the portrait revealed some hidden relation, something in the eyes, something angelic and abstract, the thing that had always aroused him in Luka and frightened him in Manolis.

He didn't drink all day, and didn't go outside a single time.

Around noon he sat down in an armchair directly beneath the portrait and ate a hard-boiled egg, gazing steadily at Manolis, who was forever raising that cigarette to his mouth. Mark ate his egg so slowly that by the time he reached the yolk the sun had set.

That night he went out and raped a boy who had been sent to the corner store for yogurt. Mark pushed him down behind his house, in front of the church gate, and the yogurt fell into the churchyard. The rape was brutal: the child kept pleading with Mark to let him go until Mark grabbed him by the hair and pounded his head several times against the cobblestones, and the child stopped screaming and pressed his cheek against the cold stone and sobbed, whimpering for his mother and swallowing his snot.

The child was nine years old. The whole time Mark was on top of him the boy kept his fist clenched tightly around an eraser he had just bought along with the yogurt, a pink, elephant-shaped eraser that smelled like candy—and despite his pain and terror, he didn't open his fist a single time for fear of losing it, though with both hands he could have fought back, could perhaps even have gotten away.

8

Manolis was heading the investigation into the murder of Alex Kopesky. All the foreigners were called in. Since Alex had been a close friend, they were all suspects.

Every day they took turns going in and sitting across from Manolis, who offered them Camels and coffee. He always had a vase of gardenias on his desk.

"Name?"

"Maggie Epstein."

"Profession?"

"Novelist."

"Cigarette?"

"No."

"Coffee?"

"Please, with sugar."

"About the murder…" Maggie would begin, but Manolis always cut her off.

"Let's not worry about the murder just now, there are much more interesting things for us to talk about." And he would speak to her about art, painting, the spring. He was supposed to be investigating Kopesky's death, but Manolis never mentioned the case to any of them. "I want to get to know you all," he would say, and offered them gardenias.

None of them had an alibi, and their statements changed from one day to the next. Their visits to the station weren't interrogations so much as social calls. They all liked going to see Manolis. It was spring and sunlight flooded his office and Manolis would toss his head back and laugh, or open the window and say, "Look at the mountains, they're covered with daisies," and Maggie or Ron or Placido would watch him, intoxicated by his liveliness, his radiance. Everyone adored him. The other policemen at the station were always making him coffee, the cleaning lady left sweets on his desk every morning, kids ran after him on the waterfront, gazing in awe at his uniform. No one could remember when Manolis had first come to work at the station on the island. It was as if he had appeared just recently, with the spring—no one could remember having seen him that winter.

As soon as Alan or Placido came in, Manolis would stand up, pull his revolver from the holster that always hung from his belt, and lay it beside the gardenias. No one could tell if it was simply an act of courtesy, or if it concealed some threat. Sometimes when he looked at them his eyes would fill with something ancient, a kind of weariness—but it was always so fleeting, and the atmosphere in his office was so pleasant that they started quarreling about whose turn it was to go. Once Alan went two days in a row and Maggie got mad and didn't invite him to dinner. On the second day Alan stayed all morning, and he and Manolis smoked three packs of Camels.

"You're a journalist?"

"Yes, but my real dream is to write a novel, that's why I came to the island, because this place has something so... how can I describe it... something so..."

"Metaphysical?" Manolis laughed. "That word has become all the rage. You haven't noticed?"

No, Alan hadn't noticed. On the contrary, "metaphysical" was a word he never heard, but Manolis was so convincing, he was probably right— yes, of course he was right, sitting there with his hands in his pockets and a cigarette dangling from his mouth, leaning back in his chair, his head resting against the wall.

He's handsome, Alan thought. *He's very handsome.*

"Yes, they all come to the island, shut themselves up with a typewriter and paper, and write page after page of bullshit. You haven't noticed that, either?"

Manolis was still laughing as Alan left the station at a run—he could even hear him laughing from the street. At home, his eyes fell on the paper and the typewriter. He ran to the bar and drank himself blind, and for a whole week didn't sober up once.

As soon as Mark entered the office, he saw the child's eraser sitting on the desk next to the gardenias. Manolis held out a pack of Camels and they smoked in silence.

"I finished your portrait," Mark said.

Manolis shifted the eraser slightly.

"I know. I'd like to see it."

"I've been painting you for years, but I only realized it was you when I saw you the other day during the parade."

"I'd like to see it." Manolis shifted the eraser again.

"It's the best piece I've ever done. With that portrait I finally accomplished absolute self-expression; it represents the culmination of all my work. Now there's nothing left for me to do."

"I know." Manolis put the eraser in Mark's palm.

"What's this?"

"It's an elephant the boy who was raped in your neighborhood was holding. Do you have any idea who it might have been?"

"No."

"Do you know anything about Kopesky's murder?"

"No. Do you?"

And so the questioning came to an end.

9

The day after Kopesky died, Alana ate Luka's pen. She chewed it up and dropped it at Luka's feet as if it were a little animal she had killed, then ran to play with her ball. Luka cried over the pen for a long time. Then she buried it in the garden and put up a cross that read, *Montblanc. Model 1967.*

For the first time, Luka went down to the harbor while it was still morning. It was raining, just as it had been the day before during the parade, but she sat outside at one of the cafés and ordered tea, the empty tables around her dripping with rain. A few teenage boys who were sitting inside stood up now and then to press their noses against the glass and stare at her. Some of them were handsome, particularly the one she often saw dancing to disco music on a yellow caique anchored at the harbor. Now he was smoking and watching her through the café window. A construction worker sitting beside him, wearing a gold chain and a pink shirt that was drenched with rain and clung to his chest, pointed at Luka and said something to the boy, and they laughed. Luka turned her chair to face the sea. She thought again of her pen, how much she had treasured it and how much she hated Alana, who was sitting beside her. What would she do without that pen? What else would she hold in her hand as she repeated the phrase "I have to write" a hundred times? Each day she'd filled the pen and set it down beside her blank sheets of paper, and it had always seemed ready, just waiting for her to begin. Now the rain was falling into her cup, her tea overflowed and started dripping onto her shoes, and the slice of lemon washed off the saucer and dropped onto the tuft of fur on top of Alana's head. Luka laughed. She hadn't laughed in months. She saw herself sitting there on the deserted waterfront surrounded by red canvas chairs full of mud with a cup of tea that was turning to rain, and the sadness she had been feeling over the broken pen was transformed into an overwhelming sense of relief. For the first time she truly loved her dog, and she pulled Alana into her lap and hugged her. Alana understood and hugged Luka back, putting her paws around her neck and licking her face, yelping. Alana, who had loved Luka in secret for all these months, waiting for her love to be returned, knew in her doggish mind that Luka had always hated that pen—that's why she had chewed it up. Now they stared into one another's eyes and Luka thought: *Yes, it was so perfect, always ready to write, but it didn't care how I was feeling, it was unconcerned, always swollen with ink, like a man lying in my bed, perpetually ready, but indifferent, loveless, mechanical, the seeds of some future vengeance already planted in his mind.* She felt such a sense of liberation that she stood up and started to dance with Alana under the rain, red ink coursing through her veins.

She had become both the book and the tool that would write it. She could feel each of her nails growing, she passed her tongue over each tooth and kissed her wrist, feeling as if the loss of her pen marked the beginning of an unmasking that went far, far deeper. She sang all the way home. That night she washed her hair, painted her toenails red, looked in the mirror—she hadn't in ages—and saw that she was pretty. She gathered all the pencils and markers she could find in the house and started to write. She wrote until morning, the way she used to, only better. The older and more chewed a pencil was, the thinner and more faded a marker's line, the faster she wrote, the more perfect the words, the more certain.

When she finally went to bed, she kept raising her head every now and then to look at the papers on her desk. Whenever she was on the verge of falling asleep, she would look again, and when she closed her eyes she would start thinking about what would happen next. What would the main character say to the woman he wanted so badly? Would he light his cigarette and say, "Would you like to come to my place for a nightcap?" Or would he light hers and say, "It's still early, why don't we go to my place for a drink?"

But Luka didn't dream about the book. She dreamed of all the men she had ever loved. They were all acrobats in some circus, and passed before her, bowing and tipping their hats, then clambered up the ropes and performed difficult, dangerous feats high up in an empty tent with no music and no crowd, just Luka clapping alone in the front row. But there was something wrong with their faces. Each one had someone else's nose or hair. Michael had Rubin's long hands, Timothy tossed his head just like Christian, whose hair was blond instead of black, Rubin spoke French like Christian even though he was actually Norwegian. Then their faces began to whirl before her, mangled and bloody, howling, faster, closer, and there was one among them she didn't recognize. His blond hair was wet and fell down over his face, hiding it completely, and he kept telling her his name but Luka couldn't hear what he was saying. Then he tossed his hair back, revealing his face, and Luka looked at him questioningly and said, "But I know you, I know you well." And he answered, "Not unless you know my name."

The next morning she took Alana down to the harbor again. She looked at the shop windows full of jewelry, at the tables of worry beads and the racks of postcards showing the island at sunset, so red it seemed to be drowning in blood. She bought ten colored pens, walked past the boy in the yellow caique, who was dancing as he tossed fish into wooden crates. When he saw Luka he turned up the music. She sat down at the same café, in the same seat as the day before, tied Alana's leash to the leg of the chair, took out her paper, lined up the pens, took another ten from her pocket, and tried to concentrate. But her eyes kept rising from the paper. She looked at everything with such thirst, such hunger, as if she were seeing it all for the first time: men drinking coffee and lighting cigarettes, women quickly combing their hair when they thought no one was looking. But Luka was looking, insatiably: now that she was finally able to write, she allowed herself the gaze she had denied herself for so long, as punishment.

The tour boat docked, full of Japanese tourists. The cats flocked to it as they always did, limping and one-eyed, running down from the mountain, materializing from all over. They came and stood in a row in the street, waiting. The tour guide appeared with a plastic bag and threw fish bones to the cats as the Japanese snapped pictures left and right. One man bent to pet a huge tomcat with yellow stripes. It scratched his hand and the man laughed and said, "Never mind," in English, but immediately asked his wife for some iodine to put on the scratch. Another man came up to Luka, looked at the twenty colored pens on the table and asked, also in English, "How much?" "Twenty thousand dollars," Luka answered. The man gave her a suspicious look and walked away.

"You're selling pens these days? Last year you were writing books."

Luka turned and saw Byron, whom she hadn't seen since summer. He sat down beside her. They had nothing to say to one another. They had known each other since childhood, they saw each other on the island every summer, and they'd never had anything to say. Sometimes they would find themselves alone together in the bar and would just sit there without speaking. This year Luka had noticed a nice watch on Byron's wrist, one of those plastic ones that were all the rage, pale blue, and all summer long she hadn't even been able to tell him how much she liked his watch.

"Should we have dinner tonight?"

"Sure," Luka said, and smiled at him. "I really like your watch."

They went to a French restaurant. There was Japanese music playing, the waiters were black, the owner was Swiss. Byron smoked Dunhills constantly. He had a childish mouth that always seemed to be frowning, as if his parents had said he couldn't go to the movies. His face was handsome, thin, sort of uncertain. They looked at one another but still had nothing to say, they just drank their champagne and ate their lobster.

Luka tried to think of something to say about lobster. That it was red? That she liked it better than shrimp? Or, on the contrary, that she preferred shrimp, though lobster was generally considered to have a subtler flavor, particularly when grilled? Byron kept lighting one Dunhill after another, until Luka had compared all kinds of shellfish in her head, the different ways they were prepared, the times of year when you could find them fresh in the market, their colors and sizes. It was midnight. Suddenly Byron looked at her with such rage in his eyes that for a moment Luka thought he would hit her, or get up and leave. Then the dam broke. She stretched her face toward his, touched his mouth with her fingers, forgot all about shellfish, and started speaking to him hurriedly, violently.

"Byron, when I'm writing, I can hear Kyria Theodora next door. For thirty years she lived up on the mountain with her goats and her sheep and her husband Stamatis. They moved down into town this year. My window looks onto her garden. Kyria Theodora shouts a lot, because for thirty years all she ever said was, 'Stamatis! Let them out of the pen!' or 'Stamatis! Put them in the pen!' Now, from all that shouting, her blood pressure is sky high, and her voice just keeps getting louder. Her mother-in-law lives with them, she's eighty-nine years old and she's dying. Each day she has visitors who sit in a circle around her talking about what'll happen when she finally dies. 'Angeliki,' they ask her, 'which cemetery do you want to be buried in, the one on the mountain or the one by the sea with the view?' 'I don't know,' Angeliki answers, and then she starts to worry because she still hasn't made up her mind. When she asks Kyria Theodora for a little more milk, her daughter-in-law shouts, 'You drank your milk, there's no more, and besides, soon enough you won't need it, or anything else!' The old woman says, 'I'm dying,' and Kyria Theodora shouts, 'You're doing just fine! Do you know what its like to have a blood pressure of twenty-two?' The old woman says, 'I'm hungry,' and Kyria Theodora shouts, 'You ate, you drank, you're done!' Do you understand, Byron?"

By now Luka was sweating. Byron wiped her forehead with his handkerchief, then touched her mouth lightly with his fingers.

"When I was working as a general manager on the cruise ships," he said, "I used to screw all the women. They would all tell me what faithful wives they were, one was on her way to Sydney to see her husband, another to Cape Town, they were always telling me how much they loved their husbands. In the afternoon while we were drinking at the bar they would show me photographs of their kids, then at night they would show up at my cabin. The next morning at breakfast, after we'd screwed all night long and I could see the hickeys and bite marks on their necks, they would tell me again what faithful wives they were, they didn't know how such a thing could have happened, they must have had too much to drink. That night they would show up at my cabin again. When we reached the port, their husbands would be waiting with bouquets of flowers and would thank me for taking such good care of their wives. All during the voyage, every evening in the ballroom they would grab me to dance. They wore brocade dresses and would rub up against me, and my nails would get caught in the fabric—I could kill them for that alone—and at night in my cabin, they would rip open their dresses with a sound like chalk on a blackboard, and would shout, 'I'm coming! I'm coming!' And the boat would rock and I would feel like throwing up."

At his house he undressed her and lay her down on a rug by the fireplace. The rug was bristly and made her back itch.

"I always knew I would conquer you one day."

"Just like the ladies on the cruise ship."

"No. Like the ladies on the island. I've wanted you for a long time. You're always sort of absent-minded, like you're in a hurry, and I like how you bite your nails and dress like a bag lady."

Later, he said, "I didn't expect you to be so tender, so warm." Much later, "It was never like that before." Then, toward morning, "With you I could do it constantly, all the time, night and day, without ever stopping." And as the sun rose, "It was never like that before." In the morning Byron made coffee and for the first time they actually talked, they smoked and talked for hours, but only about what they had just experienced: a movement, a particular kiss, the hours they had lain on their sides, hands wrapped tightly around one another's neck, kissing only on the mouth. The next day she went to his house again. This time when they lay down on the rug, their bodies were already familiar. "Perhaps because we didn't talk all those years our bodies were free to love one another from a distance," Luka said, and their limbs loved one another and Byron pressed his palm hard against her hip and asked, "Does that hurt?" and when Luka said, "Yes," he pressed even harder and asked her, "Has anyone ever hurt you like this before?" and Luka said, "No," as the sun rose. When she went home, she found a huge, hairy spider on her bed and killed it without being the least bit scared, though she was usually terrified of spiders. She felt deeply grateful to Byron. Because he had loved her that way, she would never again be afraid of spiders. But she would never tell him that. To do so would give him the power he was expecting when he asked her, "Does that hurt?" No, the spider would be her secret.

"Does that hurt?" he asked again on the third night, and on the fourth night he hurt her a lot.

On the fifth day it rained, and Luka was called to the police station. The investigations into Kopesky's murder had begun. She wanted to get it over with early so she could go to Byron's. There was nothing else she wanted to have happen that day. The only thing she could imagine herself doing was running up the stairs to his house.

At the station she sat on a bench and waited with her eyes closed, picturing the rug in front of the fireplace, trying to remember its complex patterns and colors. Then they called her name and showed her into an office. Someone was sitting behind the desk. *But I know him, I know him well.* She was afraid. His blond hair was wet, he kept telling her his name but she couldn't hear, the unfamiliar face from her dream was shouting his name at her, over and over.

"My name is Manolis."

Luka sat in a chair, suddenly very tired. She forgot all about Byron. The terror of true love was beginning.

10

Luka looked at her papers. The chewed pencils and dried-up markers had passed over the pages without leaving a trace. Here and there a letter showed, the end of a word. But they only made the page look emptier, whiter. She closed her eyes, touched her fingers to the page and tried to feel her way to some phrase, a period, a comma. But there was nothing there. She leaned her cheek against the paper and started to sob. As she cried for her invisible book, she noticed that the paper was absorbing her tears, and it occurred to her that it was probably cheap paper, though Makis at the corner store had sworn it was top quality. Then she felt ashamed. She remembered something she had once seen at a hospital. A fat old woman at a pay phone was telling some relative that a loved one had died. And though she sobbed and howled and said she would die of grief, as soon as the conversation was over, she hung up, then stuck her fingers into the slot to see if her coin had dropped through.

11

"Flying Dolphin!"

Alan leaped out of bed. It was a quarter to seven and he had missed the boat. He had packed his bags and dressed for the trip the night before; though it was May he'd even put on his Burberry raincoat so as to be completely ready. Then he'd sat on his bed smoking and drinking coffee, listening as the churchbells marked the hours, counting them as they passed, holding his watch up to his ear to make sure it hadn't stopped. He saw the whole night pass before his window, heard the first owl of the year, talked to himself for hours on end—and that made him laugh, because in the novel he was writing he'd been trying to write an interior monologue, and though he knew its mechanics and had studied other writers to see how and when they used it, he just couldn't make it work. As soon as the main character started in on his mono-logue, he seemed like the waiter at Antonio's café calling, "Ice cream! Ice cream!" to the Japanese tourists as they climbed down the gangway of their boat. "And now here I am," he said, "alone in the night, creating an interior monologue that I'll never be able to write."

Alan drank coffee and smoked, stared out the window and said, "Oh, island, I adore you, but I hate you, too! You're a prison smothered in flowers, I've never been more eager to leave a place behind. I can't stand this enchantment anymore, I can't stand being bewitched like this—when I look at you, my gaze turns to nothing but a mirror of light, I'll stare at you hypnotized for ages, and when I stop seeing you I'll feel you, and when I stop feeling you I'll die. I have such a craving for ugliness and filth, for cities, streets, cars, I want to wake up in the morning and wait at a red light to cross the street, I want to watch buses pass by, faces peering at me through the glass, and the light will turn green and I'll walk calmly over the white lines of the crosswalk. By this time tomorrow I'll be walking down city streets. I'll have escaped."

At around five he lay down for a minute and fell asleep. The next thing he knew, Heracles was calling "Flying Dolphin!" He ran to the window and saw the first hydrofoil of the day glide into the harbor and leave again right away, lifting its wings like some huge metal insect and disappearing around the cape. He was gripped by such panic that as he grabbed his suitcases and ran for the door, he picked up the coffee pot, too, and when he reached the café on the waterfront he set it down on the table, still full, the coffee still hot. It was five past seven. Heracles was on the wharf, talking to the port officer. Alan called them over to his table and offered them coffee, trying to butter them up—especially Heracles, who in Alan's mind had become the god of the hydrofoil, crying "Flying Dolphin!" in a playful, sing-song voice, as if he were in a one-man show on Broadway.

The port officer took two paper cups from a trash can attached to a utility pole. The can had *Rubishes* written on the side.

"They're clean," he said. "I put them there every night after they empty the trash, so in the morning I can have my coffee or orange juice whenever I want." They sat down, poured themselves coffee, lit cigarettes. They were alone on the waterfront; all the cafés were closed, the sun still hidden behind the mountain.

"You brought the coffee, we've got the cups— that's what I call organization," Heracles said in all seriousness, then fell silent.

I better watch it or I'll go mad, or burst out laughing, Alan thought, then asked when the next boat was.

"Is your hair naturally blond or do you bleach it?" Heracles asked. "My wife's hair is sort of blond and one day she put bleach on it and sat in the sun and she ended up with hair as orange as a carrot."

"It's natural," said Alan.

"My wife's an idiot," Heracles said, then fell silent again. Then he remembered Alan's question and exchanged glances with the port officer. They pulled some papers from their pockets and spread them out on the table.

"What's today's date?"

"May 2," the port officer answered.

Heracles looked at his sheet.

"Middle season ends in May but it doesn't say what day."

The port officer looked at his sheet.

"No. High season starts in May, so by May 2 we should already be in high season, in which case the schedules change. Sorry, Mr. Alan, today is a tough call as far as the times are concerned. But I'm sure we're in high season by now."

Annoyed, Heracles rustled his papers and underlined something with a red marker.

"No. High season starts *in* May, but we don't know what day, so that means it's still middle season but almost high season, we're heading toward high season—here, Mr. Alan, look for yourself, to me it's perfectly clear, there's no question about it."

Alan saw the sun rising from behind the mountain. He was sweating and his hands were shaking, though he hadn't had a thing to drink.

"What time is the next boat? I demand to know what time the next boat leaves."

"There's no way of telling," Heracles said, "since we don't know if—"

"Yes," said Alan. "I get it, Heracles, you don't need to tell me again—but goddammit, when's the next boat?"

"No way of telling, Mr. Alan, and there's no need to curse so early in the morning, is it our fault if we don't know whether—"

"Oh, shut up!"

The three English words echoed loudly on the deserted waterfront.

"Excuse me," Alan said, also in English.

"Never mind," Heracles replied. They were the only words he knew in English, and he was always happy to get a chance to use them. He nodded to the port officer and they rose.

"*Bon voyage*," the port officer told Alan. He had learned that from a Japanese girl he had gotten alone in an alleyway the whole time her boat was docked was there. Afterward she took a picture of him from the boat and shouted, "*Bon voyage!*"

"What does that mean?" he had asked a mule driver.

"Have a nice trip."

"Why is she telling me '*Bon voyage*' when she's the one leaving?"

"Who cares?" the mule driver had said. "You screwed her, right? So yell a '*Bon voyage*' back and that's that."

Heracles and the port officer left.

Day was breaking over the empty waterfront. Alan sat waiting with his bags clenched between his legs, his raincoat buttoned up to his throat, his belt tight. The pot on the table was still full of hot coffee and the sea was empty, not even a caique passed by, and the sun lit up the mountains, which were covered in daisies and poppies—and Alan remembered that it was spring and for a moment he felt that love again, that desire for the island, the same love that always choked him back in Australia whenever he remembered a particular street or smell.

"At least you were spared the low season schedules," someone behind him said, and laughed. He turned his head and saw Manolis, impeccable in his uniform, looking at him conspiratorially, about to start laughing again—and the look in his eyes was so lively that Alan leaned back in his chair and began to laugh uncontrollably, the laughter he had been holding in for so long, until both of them were shaking with silent laughter. "*Bon voyage*," Alan said in his Australian accent and they laughed even harder. Then Alan unbuttoned his raincoat and tossed it over his bags.

"Speaking of high season, why don't we go for a highball at the bar?"

"It's too early, the bar is closed," Manolis said. "But Antonio should be opening soon, we can go there for a brandy."

"What's wrong with me today? It's as if I've already left and have forgotten everything about this place. For months now I've been opening the bar at noon. I'm Bill's partner now, I bought Stephanos's share when he went into detox. You didn't know? I don't want brandy, I want to get on that boat and leave."

"I wouldn't worry about that. The boats come all the time, we just don't know exactly when. Why don't we sit here and have a few drinks and as soon as we see it..." Manolis pulled a slip of paper from his pocket and read, in English, "off you go!"

Alan laughed again.

"Where'd you learn that?"

"At the station. From you guys. Aren't I always having to deal with foreigners? So I write it all down on a sheet of paper. I learned the slang too, listen: 'what the fuck,' 'screw you, bastard,' 'motherfucker,' 'faggot,' that's better than 'queer,' or at least that's what one guy told me, this black guy with orange hair, this six-foot faggot who tried to strangle me one night at the station—which do you like better, 'fag,' 'faggot,' or the French '*pédé*?"

"'Homosexual.'"

"You're right. It's more respectful." Manolis winked at him. "Anyhow, you're quite a lady's man yourself, three marriages, and I've met all your wives, they were gorgeous, blonde, Nordic, just my type— and I've seen you with other women, too, real lookers, you put us all to shame. Do you take them back to your place after the bar?"

"Of course. Where else would I take them?"

"It's just that a few times you seemed to be saying goodnight to them at the door. Could happen. Anyhow, I always say you're a lady's man, the construction workers and mule drivers can say what they like, as far as they're concerned all foreigners are faggots because they're polite and have manners, but I always say you may be Australian, but you're a lady's man, and a writer too, just like…" Manolis pulled out his slip of paper again. "Hemingway, writer and journalist, just like you. Nobel Prize. Shot his brains out with a rifle at his house in the country. Had a beard."

Manolis put the paper back in his pocket. They smoked in silence. It was five past eight.

"This island is full of writers," Manolis suddenly continued, as if it was something he'd been thinking about. "They all come here and drive themselves crazy, this one can't write, that one can't stop, they all go nuts in the end. If you asked me to make you a story, to sit there for hours writing it down with all those details, how this guy smokes, how that guy dresses, what they're all feeling—there's no way I could do it. How can you write down what some-one's feeling? We don't even know in real life, a mood can change in a split second. By the time I've finished a cigarette, I can't even remember what I was thinking when I lit it. And you writers want to capture all that on a sheet of paper, and for it to have some kind of meaning, too. Why do you put your-selves through all that? That's why the whole lot of you are always drunk, and one guy goes and kills himself like Mr. Ernest Nobel Hemingway, and you're always trying to get away—why don't you guys just write letters or something if you need to blow off some steam? The island's a perfect place for writing letters. Me, I write my reports with nice colored pens, put in a little emotion, and that's that."

"How do you know all that?"

Manolis's face grew soft, changed, his mouth shaping itself into an unfamiliar curve.

He has the face of an intellectual, Alan thought, so surprised that he didn't even hear Manolis's reply: "I learned from Luka." And when Alan looked again, it seemed as if he had imagined everything. Manolis's face was the same as it always was, once again on the verge of laughter. *I can write novels everywhere except on the page*, Alan thought. *I even want to turn this cop into a great thinker. And he writes his reports with nice pens.*

Alan laughed. "How come you never answer questions? How do you know so much about writers and what they go through?"

Manolis laughed, clapped Alan on the shoulder, and again assumed his conspiratorial air. "Because, my friend, I always ask the questions. I'm a cop, remember? Look! Finally! Antonio's is open. Yiorgos! Two brandies and two espressos."

Alan felt better after the brandy. He hadn't had a drink in days; he had decided that his intense desire to leave the island demanded complete abstinence from alcohol, because when he drank he had no desires, only nostalgia, and nostalgia wasn't enough to make him pack his bags and go. But with the first brandy he relaxed and saw how ridiculous his anxiety over the boat schedule had been. He looked at

Manolis, who was smoking, staring at the sea absent-mindedly, as if preoccupied. *He's a fool*, Alan thought. *He seems smart because he's so handsome, but he's really just a cop, a villager who pulls out his little sheet of foreign words, like the baker making change for German tourists—that face, those eyes fool us all into thinking he's something he's not, and we sit there and talk to him about literature. It's his eyes, and those unbelievable cheekbones, and the blond hair, as if he just stepped out of some Russian novel, he looks like Vronsky but he's just a small-town cop, an idiot, and I'm sitting here drinking brandy with him. It's the island's fault, even Kostas at the post office, when he pulls his glasses down to the tip of his nose and says to me, 'Let's see, Mr. Alan, if we have anything in Post Restante today'—even Kostas reminds me of a young Trotsky…*

"Yiorgos! Two brandies!" Manolis shouted. It was a quarter past nine and by now there were a few other customers, parents eating breakfast while their kids fed buttered bread to the cats. Yiorgos shouted the first "Ice cream!" of the day, and Pantelis showed up with Killer, his German shepherd, and led it to the other end of the wharf for its training, as he did every morning. They were both gigantic and walked in exactly the same way. Every morning at a quarter past nine they came down for Killer's training, which lasted all of three minutes. Alan watched from a distance as Pantelis unleashed the dog and raised his hand in the air. The dog immediately lay down. Then Pantelis walked off and the dog stayed there, head on its paws, until Pantelis reached the other end of the wharf, stopped, turned around, and lowered his hand. The dog sprang up, rushed toward him, stopped, sat down, and held out its paw. Pantelis put its leash on and they walked back toward Antonio's. On the way, Pantelis would stop abruptly in the road, and the dog would stop too; they started and stopped, and Pantelis bent and stroked its head. A crowd had gathered in front of the bakery. Pantelis pointed at someone and said, "That one, Killer!" Then the dog went wild, rearing up on its hind legs. Its face became a mask, its lips curled back toward its eyes as it bared its glistening, blinding white teeth. The crowd that had gathered stepped back, laughing, and Pantelis said, "If I didn't train him, he'd tear you all to shreds!" Then he bought the dog a tiropita and they started slowly toward home, both of them shaking the heavy chain to make noise.

This daily repetition of the same scenes at the same time had given Alan a taste of the timeless, the eternal, something he was trying to express in his book, but which he really only felt when he saw Pantelis leading Killer down to the wharf. Sitting at his typewriter, he was incapable of conveying that feeling. But today, since it was the last time he would be seeing this ritual, it seemed different to him— unique, no longer timeless but utterly local. The whole island suddenly took on the sheen of the singular, the never-to-be-repeated. He was leaving, and so he became the outside gaze, finally in charge, having conquered the island that had almost killed him—and so he loved it again, with his whole heart, as the repetition became already a memory. He had been saved.

"Yiorgos, two brandies!"

It was ten in the morning and Alan wanted to treat Manolis to one last drink, since he would be leaving soon and wouldn't be seeing him again.

"Manolis, I really like you."

"And I love you, Alan."

Manolis's voice seemed sad. *Because I'm leaving*, Alan thought.

"To our health!"

Alan downed his drink in a single swallow. He saw Heracles standing on the dock; he looked all misty, as if Alan were seeing him from a distance through dirty binoculars. Heracles's hands were tentacles sinking into the sea. Alan tried to call to him, but his mouth was numb. Manolis stood up and walked over to Heracles, and to Alan they seemed to be talking for hours. Every now and then Heracles would point out to sea, throw his hands in the air, pull the schedule from his pocket, and slap the paper angrily with his palm; then both of them would turn and look at Alan, and they seemed to be looking at him as if he were crazy, or sick.

I'm drunk, he thought. *I have to stop, drink some coffee, splash some water on my face.* He saw Yiorgos passing with a tray of ice cream decorated with little flags and sparklers. "An espresso," he said, but Yiorgos didn't hear him, or perhaps Alan had just thought the words and hadn't said them at all. "An espresso," he said again, but by now Yiorgos was too far away to hear.

Manolis came back.

"Heracles told me the next boat isn't until two."

"So why are you so happy?"

"I'm not happy. You're drunk. Why don't we go to the bar to drop off your bags and wait?"

"But it's morning. The bar is closed."

"No, it's noon, and you're smashed," Manolis said, laughing, then picked up Alan's suitcases. "Come on."

When they got to the bar Alan took out his key and unlocked the door. "Here I am as usual, opening the bar at noon, and no one knows I'm about to leave—just you, me, and the bags."

He switched on the fans and put some Vivaldi on the stereo. Outside the sun beat down but inside it was cool and dark. Alan went behind the bar and took down the cocktail shaker.

"How do you want your drink, with vodka or tequila?"

"Tequila." Manolis sunk into the red cushions and lit a cigarette. Alan pulled various bottles down from the shelves, whistling along with the Vivaldi. He poured the shots into the shaker carefully and shook it like a pro. The high, lively notes from the stereo mingled with the rhythmic sounds of the shaker and the ceiling fans.

Alan served Manolis with a bow.

"I hope it meets with your satisfaction, sir."

Manolis took a sip. "It's perfect," he said in English.

He leaned back into the cushions again, tossing his Camels and lighter onto the table. The Vivaldi had reached the apex of joy, the eruption of spring. Manolis gazed at the fans on the ceiling, a cigarette in his mouth, hands behind his head. Alan took his glass and sat down in a chair across from him, and Manolis closed his eyes.

I should be at the dock, Alan thought, but the waterfront seemed hours away, so he went back behind the bar and fixed two Bloody Marys. Manolis lit another cigarette, this time with his eyes closed, as the music stopped.

Alan turned and looked at the big mirror behind the bottles and saw Manolis sunk in the red cushions, his jacket open and the top three buttons of his shirt undone—and that uniform, worn so casually, lent him a frightening air of absolute power. Alan had another drink, and the image in the mirror blurred; all he could see was Manolis's blond hair against the cushions. He started talking into the mirror, because that way he could talk to Manolis and himself and the bottles and to the mountain that sprang up behind them, and the bottles looked like trees on the mountain, and Manolis had stretched out to sleep in a valley of red.

"I'll never be a real writer, major or minor, because I always write in moments of exaltation, so I always just write about myself instead of entering into my characters and becoming the tool that brings them to life. That's why I can never really express a situation, a mood, a change. I'll never be able to communicate that certain something, that nothing, that vertigo in the text that comes from somewhere but you don't know where, whether it's the sentences on the page or something prior to them. It's as if the words have shot from somewhere like comets and collided with the page, wounding it with the dizzying speed of their fall. Writing should be something cold, detached, like a comet—but I'm such an idiot that I write with my heart. It's the only reserve I've got, I've turned all my thoughts into feelings, and now when I sit down to write, I use my pain crudely, coarsely, not to nourish my work, but as my sole source of inspiration—so that pain keeps bringing me back to myself, because I don't use it to strengthen my characters, but to empty them of all feeling, all suffering, since the only suffering I really care about is my own. Of course you'll say if I know all this, why don't I do something about it. It takes more, old boy, it takes more. Sometimes I imagine and even long for a violent death that might put me, just for a second, into that state of writing, so that just for a second"—

Alan hurled his glass at the mirror—"I might finally feel like a goddamn fucking writer!"

Manolis clapped slowly, three times.

"Better than the theater."

Alan turned and looked at him, crying. "Idiot," he said. "Idiot, idiot, idiot."

"Flying Dolphin!"

Manolis sat motionless as the ceiling fans spun. Alan rushed for the door but fell flat on his face on a table, hands and feet making strange motions as if he were trying to swim his way to the harbor. Manolis closed his eyes as the fan on the right started squeaking slightly, as it always did.

"Flying Dolphin!" Heracles's voice seemed to be coming from the mountain. Through the windows and in the mirror, the mountain seemed enormous, close. It was all you could see, and the graveyard where a single grave stood out clearly from the rest. Alan lay down on the cushions and fell asleep.

He dreamed that the Flying Dolphin flew into the bar as if coming into the harbor; it tore through the walls, its prow crashed into the mirror with terrifying speed, smashing the bottles. Alan was climbing on board with his suitcases when he heard a voice: "Excuse me, sir, your dog isn't muzzled." "But I don't have a dog!" he shouted. "I'm afraid it can't come on board without a muzzle," the voice answered. "But there's no dog, I don't have a dog!" he kept protesting as everyone pushed past him onto the boat and the

Flying Dolphin unstuck its prow from the mirror, which shattered noiselessly and fell in splinters to the ground. The boat backed out of the bar, turned around in the yard, and instead of heading out to sea, flew up and vanished into the sky.

When Alan woke up, Manolis was behind the bar, fixing cocktails and whistling Vivaldi. Suddenly Alan hated him. *I've never talked that way to anyone before—since I know I'll never see him again, I talked to him the way you might talk to a prostitute.* He was sober now, and had once again been seized by an insane desire to leave. How had he ended up at the bar, how had he let the hours pass, how had he missed the boat when he'd stayed up waiting all night long with his pot of coffee and his Burberry raincoat?

"The next boat is at a quarter to four, I called Heracles while you were sleeping." Manolis handed Alan a glass, and raised his own: "To the Flying Dolphins!"

"I don't want another drink. Let's go."

All the tables at Antonio's were full.

"Ice cream, espresso, omelet!" Yiorgos shouted, always in English.

Manolis carried the luggage into the café. "Keep an eye on these," he told one of the waiters, "especially the typewriter." He took Alan by the arm and they walked together toward the bakery.

"There's no way we can hang around here until four. Let's go to the Hydronetta and get some sun.

You can take a last look at the sea. I'll keep an eye on the time, you won't miss the next one."

They sat in canvas chairs on one of the upper levels of the Hydronetta, a café that spilled down a set of platforms leading to the sea. The cliff was at their feet, and before them the water shone and the air was so clear they could see all the islands in the distance, as snatches of Steely Dan came drifting over from the bar to their right. The rock music was oddly suited to the light and the blue of the sea: the saxophone slapped the waves roughly and came back on Alan with such violence it was as if someone were hitting his face and neck. The landscape, which he was used to thinking of as peaceful and quiet, had turned into some kind of monstrous beast wrestling with the music. The islands, the sea, the sky all danced to Steely Dan, as the saxophone stroked them gently, or hit them—and Alan, who had always imagined this view accompanied by Bach, now saw that the landscape didn't want Bach, it loved violence and Steely Dan. The island seemed to be mocking him, like a woman you always thought of as distant and romantic who goes and throws herself at you in some dark alley.

Beside him, Manolis was gazing at the sea, his eyes two slits. A group of teenage boys came out of the bar, set their drinks on a table and stripped down to their bathing suits, then gathered at the top of the stairs, smoking Marlboros. One of them, thin and blond, also seemed to have been touched by the strange marriage of landscape and music: his sensitive face had something aggressive about it, his blue eyes had a metallic gaze, intense and indifferent, and his skin seemed somehow both smooth and coarse. His suit drooped a bit around his waist, showing a belt of white skin that had yet to be touched by the sun. The boy kept running his hand over that stretch of skin, stopping to trace circles around his belly button with his finger. He turned and looked at Alan. He smiled, continuing the motion. Then he said something to one of the other boys and they ran down the stairs and plunged joyously into the water, shouting and laughing, diving and wrestling. Again the blond boy raised his head and looked at Alan. He seemed to be nodding hello or inviting him to join them. Alan turned and looked at Manolis. His eyes were closed, perhaps he was sleeping. The music grew louder, the sun beat down, the boys came running up the stairs shaking the water from their hair, their bodies glistening in the sun. Manolis opened his eyes. *The drops of water in their belly buttons must be full of salt*, Alan thought. Suddenly he felt very thirsty—and in order to escape that thirst, which made him anxious and impatient, he thought hard about Debby, who was waiting for him back in Sydney. He had sent her a telegram that read, *I love you*. He had never brought Debby to the island. "You'll only be able to write if you're with me," she always told him. "You'll have peace and quiet, you'll quit drinking, we'll have a few friends over in the evenings, nothing more." She described this "writer's life" as if reading the stage directions for some play, or repeating something she had read in *Home and Garden* magazine: the office with the plants, the vase of roses at the far right edge of the desk, which would be placed at an angle so the light would fall on it from the window to the left, the red typewriter, the stack of white paper beside it. Whenever she started talking like that Alan would be seized by panic. He'd never be able to write in a room like that, not even a letter to his mother, he would go in every morning in his clean silk robe and as soon as he closed the door the room would become the writer, and he an intruder, an interloper. Whenever Debby spoke to him of that sunlit room Alan couldn't help imagining Balzac's stained silk robe, his darkened room, the pot of coffee perpetually kept warm on the stove, and that endless night with the curtains drawn and Balzac's hand running constantly over the page— because nighttime and coffee were precisely the things that, as Balzac himself had written, "make ideas come galloping." And with that image and that image alone, Alan's longing for those secret hours of writing became uncontrollably immense, as if his whole body were lighting up, as if his insides were catching fire, as if he were having an allergic reaction and would die if he didn't find an antidote and the only antidote was writing, was the text that kept slipping away, leaving him with nothing but the image of Balzac, which kept expanding, growing bigger, humming inside his head—and then Alan desperately needed a drink.

Now, watching the boys stretch their long young limbs in the sun, all that came back to him—Debby waiting for him with the red typewriter, Balzac's hand galloping in the night—and his whole body caught fire. He rose and ran to the bar.

"Two glasses of vodka with lots of ice."

When the barman had fixed the drinks, Alan downed them right there at the bar, and then a third, and when he sat down again in the sun he drank the fourth in a single swallow as the sounds of the saxophone poured over the boys' naked limbs. Manolis sipped his vodka slowly, staring at the same spot in the sea as if turning something over in his mind, as if he had forgotten all about Alan. But Alan didn't care, nothing could bother him now. He got up and came back with a bottle of vodka and more ice, quickly drank half the bottle, and then, with exaggerated care, dropped a few ice cubes into his glass and poured the vodka over it just as he had at the bar. Then, staggering, he got up and shifted his chair so as to have a better view of the boys.

"Don't stare. They know me. Yesterday the blond one you've been drooling over came to the station to turn in a wallet he found on the rocks. He remembers me, and now he's watching me—so cool it, or put on your sunglasses."

"I'm not looking at them. I'm looking at the sea. And if I do happen to be looking their way, it's because they're part of the landscape. You're going to call me a faggot now, too?"

"But you are one."

Alan's glass broke; the shards fell slowly over the cliff.

"I could kill you for what you just said."

"If only," Manolis said tenderly. "If only."

"Flying Dolphin!"

Heracles' voice stretched over the sea, mingling with the saxophone. It sounded like a woman's voice, like someone singing a song or reciting a poem called "Flying Dolphin." They didn't say anything, just listened as the hydrofoil's wings lifted again; then the noise vanished.

The blond boy left his friends and came over to where they were sitting. He stopped in front of Alan and put a cigarette in his mouth.

"Got a light?"

Alan looked at the white belt of skin, which was now turning pink, looked at the soft, bleached down on the boy's legs, looked at his knees, bony and bruised from soccer games, looked at his calves, thin and slightly crooked, and his eyes stopped again at the swimsuit, which had dried and clung to the boy, showing every inch of his body as if he were naked.

He was so close that if Alan had bent down, he could have licked the salt from his navel.

"Got a light?"

Alan held up his lighter. As the boy bent his head his wet hair brushed Alan's cheek. It smelled of the sea and Johnson's Baby Shampoo, his scalp of bitter honey. The lighter fell and the boy bent to pick it up. His whole body slid before Alan's mouth as he stooped, and again as he rose. He lit his cigarette and stood before Alan, waiting.

"Get lost," Manolis said.

"Why? He's yours?"

"Get lost. He's not that type."

"Are you kidding? He's been staring at me for the past two hours."

"He was looking at the scenery."

"Is that what they're calling it these days?"

"The gentleman is leaving today for Australia."

"So what's he doing here, drunk off his ass?"

"Get lost. Or I'll take you down to the station."

"You must want something from him. Or maybe he's a mafia guy and you're protecting him?"

"I'm protecting him, yes."

"Okay, Manolis. But tell him not to look at the scenery like that, someday he'll get himself in trouble."

The boy hesitated. He looked at Alan, blowing smoke out his nostrils, studying the expensive shirt, the heavy watch, the soft leather of Alan's shoes.

Then he shrugged and flashed him a smile.

"Some other time, mister," he said in English. Then he went back to his friends, dragging his feet and turning every few steps to look back.

Alan's sweat smelled of vodka and his face was a drunkard's idiotic mask. He grabbed Manolis's arm and squeezed it tightly. There was something he wanted to tell him, but instead of speaking he suddenly leaned forward and vomited over the cliff. As he watched the vomit falling into the sea like rain, Manolis felt as if he had seen this scene before, but he couldn't remember where—perhaps in a dream?

"When I get to Sydney, I'll wait at a red light to cross the street, the light will turn green—"

"Shut up already, Alan. Shut up. Shut up. Shut up."

Manolis stood up, grabbed him, pulled him to his feet.

"Let's go to the station. It'll be empty at this time of day. I'll fix you some coffee and you can pull yourself together."

Alan dozed as they walked, leaning against Manolis's shoulder. As they were entering the station, he woke up and read aloud from the gold plaque on the wall: "*Nihil Graeciae Humanius nihil Sanctius. Ouden tis Ellados Anthropinoteron, ouden Ieroteron.* Nothing more human than Greece, nothing holier."

They both laughed at his pronunciation of the Greek. The station was dark and empty. Somewhere a telephone rang. When they got to Manolis's office they left the shutters closed, turned on the fan, lit cigarettes, and settled into two chairs.

There was a vase of gardenias on the desk. "That's your weakness, those gardenias," Alan said spitefully.

"If only your weaknesses were like that," Manolis answered.

"But they are." Alan winked, and they started to laugh. An icon of Christ hung in a gold frame on the wall above the desk. Dressed in red, with yellow hair, slightly cross-eyed, cheeks puffed as if he were whistling. His finger was pointing to the telephone.

"The butcher has the same one, only his is pointing to the brisket," Alan said, and they laughed even harder.

They sat there chuckling under their breath and smoking, and every so often they would break into laughter again at the thought of the butcher's Christ. They felt close again, now that they had traveled all day and had finally reached their destination. Alan had set out on a different journey, but he had no memory of it anymore, since now, at the station, they had arrived.

They stirred slowly in their chairs, smoking, laughing for no reason, perfect conspirators. Time passed, red light filtered in through the shutters, Manolis got up and put on his jacket, Alan looked at the revolver at his waist, his slim thighs, his long legs.

He's the most beautiful man I've ever seen.

"Come on," Manolis said. "Let's go."

They went out into the narrow streets and walked for a long time until they reached some ruins high on the mountain, all wells and arches.

"I have to pee," Alan said.

"Use the well," Manolis said as he grabbed Alan, picked him up, and threw him down in front of a well. "That tickles," Alan shrieked, and now they were laughing loudly, wildly. Manolis, glued to Alan's back, reached his arms around his waist, and, whistling, ripped his pants with such force that he even tore the leather belt. Alan closed his eyes and steadied himself against the well, gripping its lip, and when Manolis came inside him he experienced such a rush of pleasure that he didn't even feel the first thrust of the knife, and the second he confused with that exquisite pain. He felt only the third, and it seemed to him that the waterfront was peeling away from the mountain and sailing off into the sea like an enormous boat blazing with lights. Now the knife thrusts came fast and dense, and the stone of the well beneath his hands was hot, like the blood that was pouring out of him, soaking into the soil. His back was a torrent of blood, though his chest remained untouched. It was how he had always dreamed it would be, the back of his body butchered, the front smooth, virginal—and in a moment of utter bliss, he saw the book he would have written now, that very instant, if he'd had time, saw the chapters weaving themselves together gracefully before his eyes, the commas, the periods giving life and breath to the words, and he felt an endless gratitude to Manolis for giving him all this, and in this way, eternally. He knelt and clung to the well, rested his cheek tenderly against the warm stone, and stopped thinking. Images, details, fragments filled his head: his coffee pot on the table at Antonio's, a green comb he'd had as a child, his first cold, Heracles's nose, a certain look in his mother's eyes—and the last thing he heard before slipping away was "Flying Dolphin!" And the sound of steely wings slicing through water.

12

Manolis loved Luka from the moment he saw her
coming into his office. The investigation into Alex
Kopesky's murder was still underway.

He had known her for years. She belonged to the
group of foreigners with their books and their paintings, their drinking bouts and their strange complicity.
Whenever a foreigner arrived on the island they
immediately swallowed him up, made him one of
them, so they all ended up resembling one another,
like brothers and sisters, as if an enormous family had
laid siege to the island, obeying some secret signal
from the ends of the earth, having chosen the island as
its final resting place, the way sick elephants gather to
die in secret clearings in the jungle.

But Manolis thought differently of Luka and
Mark, he admired them. Mark painted all day, and
Luka had written an actual book that had been translated into lots of languages, and now she was writing
a second. The others just drank and cried and used
art to disguise their hopelessness; for them art was the
last stop, their final excuse to live a little longer. They
polluted the island with foreign thoughts that the
island couldn't stand, weighed the island down with
an unbearable burden that it tried in vain to cast off.

But he always tried to protect Luka and Mark. He
knew Mark had raped the child, but he didn't tell

anyone, and one night he threw the elephant eraser into the sea. Manolis remembered Mark as he had been during the Carnival parade, sitting in the rain saying, "It doesn't matter," with the boy's head in his lap and the boy's father rushing at him with the knife; he remembered Mark telling him, "I finished your portrait"; Mark at the station staring at the eraser; Mark always drunk and with that look in his eyes, like the gaze of donkeys as they stare endlessly at the ground, tenderly, but with that stubbornness, that insolence of eternal pain. When he saw Mark that way, small and shriveled, fragile, ageless, sitting drunk on some staircase staring at the ground as endlessly as donkeys, the need to protect him welled up inside of him and he would take Mark home, put him to bed, and sit with him until he fell asleep. Mark had committed crimes and should have been arrested, but Manolis covered up for him, though he hated the others who had done nothing. Because that was precisely it—they did nothing at all, they slept all day and got disgustingly drunk at night and destroyed everything, and for Manolis that kind of disorder was worse than murder. To kill was something clean, the nostalgia for a kind of order. The kind of order the islanders maintained when they celebrated births, mourned deaths, swept the street in front of their houses, kept watch over their daughters. But lately they too had gotten caught up in this fever of disorder, and Manolis was sure the foreigners were to blame.

Now in church the islanders spoke loudly, the women wore more and more makeup, and bracelets that jangled beneath the dome; some even snuck out the back to smoke. Manolis hated disorder. His pencils were always lined up on his desk according to color, the gardenias were fresh every day, the ashtrays were always clean, his uniform always freshly ironed. He washed his hair every day and clipped and filed his nails. All this came naturally to him; it was a kind of offering he made to those around him, an act of love.

Manolis loved Luka suddenly, the moment he saw her coming into his office. When she looked at him with those glad eyes in that sad face, a shudder passed through him, like an earthquake gathering in the depths of the earth. Love sprang from inside of him with such force that it couldn't find its target, it ricocheted blindly off the walls like a tornado, sweeping up everything in its path until it finally found Luka and rushed at her headlong. Manolis looked at Luka and thought, *I love Luka.* His whole life up until that point vanished. In the blink of an eye he had entered the world of love and disorder. It scared him. They looked at one another and saw that they resembled one another, like siblings: the same eyes, the same mouth, the same hands.

They looked at one another and the immersion grew deeper, more final.

At some point Manolis closed his eyes. When he opened them, Luka was gone.

13

They had been drinking since morning at Antonio's. They had drunk the whole night before, too, at the bar. When the bar closed at five, they had gone and settled into the red chairs at Antonio's, and when he opened at seven they started ordering beers. Then they switched to wine, then to brandy. Now it was late afternoon and they were still at the same table. At first Yiorgos would come and collect the empty bottles and glasses, but the table filled up again so fast that he got tired of clearing it and started putting the new orders down wherever he could find room.

Emma, Sue's daughter, was building a tower of empty beer cans around their table. She had been sitting and playing on the ground since morning and whenever she tried to get up Sue would push her down again. "Play!" she'd tell her, "Play!"

Emma was wearing a straw hat with red roses. She was very proud of her hat. Practically the only reason she left the house was so she could show it off in front of the other kids. When Gunther, who was completely drunk, emptied his beer onto the roses, crying, "I'm watering them!"—ruining not just the hat but also her dress with the purple flowers—the other kids started laughing and sticking their tongues out at her, and Emma looked at the grownups with such hatred in her eyes that Gunther apologized.

"Fuck you all!" Emma shouted. Then she spit on Sue, threw her hat into the sea, and ran off.

Mark, watching Emma's blond hair fluttering and disappearing down an alleyway, saw his daughter Shein before him, at that age, with that same hatred in her eyes, disappearing down the very same alleyway. But he immediately pushed the image from his mind.

I promised myself I'd never think of her, I swore I'd never picture her, never—her blond hair, her smooth cheeks, her little hands with polish on just one nail—go away, Shein!

But when he was very drunk, when the alcohol in his system had reached almost deadly levels, there was no way he could push her image from his mind. He saw her so clearly that sometimes, when some other child with the same blond hair ran past, he was sure it was her.

Shein! Shein! He was running after her.

Daddy! Daddy! Shein turned, raised her arms high in the air, and ran to him, laughing, as Mark reached out to embrace her.

And here I am in the same café where I used to sit with Shein when she was a baby. And no one will ever call me Daddy again.

"I'm hungry," said Gunther. "Mark, you should eat too. You haven't eaten in days. I'll feed you. Yiorgos! One spaghetti special!"

The spaghetti came, Gunther stood and rammed a forkful into Mark's mouth, Mark spat it out onto

Sue, Sue starting shouting, Yiorgos came running.

"Enough already! If you guys keep it up, I'll kick you all out. You've been driving us crazy since morning."

Gunther, drunk and enormous, held up the plate of spaghetti.

"You see this?"

"Yes, I see it," Yiorgos said, sighing, and left.

Gunther looked at Mark again.

"Are you going to eat?"

"No."

Gunther bent over him, grabbed him by the hair, and yanked his head back.

"Mark, open your mouth."

The people at the neighboring tables were all hurrying to pay and leave.

"Your mouth, Mark! Open your mouth!"

The first forkful burned his throat. Gunther's voice disappeared. With the second bite Mark was somewhere else entirely. Waves of love rushed over him, and he closed his eyes.

Your mouth, Mark. Give me your mouth… Libbie's voice. Libbie's face over his. Their naked bodies on the bed, drenched in sun one September afternoon.

Your mouth, Mark, quick, your mouth.

He saw his mouth opening, meeting Libbie's lips, drinking in her hot spit, his insides filling with love, his whole body storing up love and asking for more, more.

"More! More!" Gunther cried. He fed Mark quickly, messily, holding his jaw open as he would a dog's to keep it from biting. With each hot mouthful, new waves of love rose up.

How much love there had been back then! Twenty, thirty years before? Even the smallest gesture was precious, he would buy bread at the bakery and it would almost bring tears to his eyes to think of Libbie eating it while it was still warm. In the afternoons they sat at the same café where he was sitting now. What was it called back then? And how many names had it gone through since? One? Two? He had carried a drawing pad with him wherever he went and was constantly sketching the island, Libbie by his side. Back then he hadn't painted headless boys. He had been in love with the island. He drew it constantly, from every angle, at every moment of the day, following the light. Back then he painted landscapes, flowers, houses, old doors, the tall grass tumbling down the mountainside to the sea; back then he loved colors, ochre and yellow and blue, he painted skies that were all the shades of violet and mauve, setting suns of royal purple. Under his hand the island was constantly being born again, more alive, more intense, and it was grateful to him for that. And Mark, painting with such adoration, slowly became an integral part of the island, almost like its shadow. At some point there had been a moment of absolute unification, a marriage between him and the island. He knew he would never leave.

How much love there had been! Perhaps those had been his strongest moments: sitting at the café with Libbie on September afternoons, not touching, not speaking, the island breathing around them. Their love had been so strong that even sex was a kind of separation. They no longer desired anything. Their passion was so great that they no longer wanted that passion. They wanted to sit as motionless as rocks and gaze out on this island which had brought them so close, embraced them with its mountain and its light and its nights.

When had the island begun to change? He couldn't remember. Perhaps when he stopped painting it. Perhaps when Libbie started going on walks by herself and coming back distracted, a new look in her eyes. Almost imperceptibly, the texture of the air changed, the light blurred, the landscape seemed oddly forsaken. It was as if the island had lost its innocence and was exhaling something shrewd or dangerous, as if that divine joy had left the island, as if it had been cursed. The island had brought them together, and now it pushed them apart.

The island had remained this way ever since, in fact over the years the sense of its cursedness had deepened. Mark knew the island well, he had been one of the first foreigners to arrive and had witnessed all the changes it had undergone. The old love had abandoned it. The island was empty. Its beauty had once been soft and rounded, but had now taken on a jagged edge—even the birds now sang with shrill, harsh notes, and the seasons changed abruptly, as if a blade were falling and dividing one from the next before they had time to complete their cycle. The island had passed through all the stages of love, indifference, and emptiness. Now it was full of hate. Mark had never experienced such hatred before. There was something deadly in it that terrified him. These days he was scared to look at the scenery he had once painted with such passion and trust. He walked with his eyes trained on the ground. He drank more and more so as to see the island blurry and undefined. It was the island that made him drink, he drank in order to make it disappear—only instead of the island, he himself was disappearing, becoming blurry, undefined.

Another forkful. Gunther's laugh. This time the wave that rose was bitter.

One summer. What year? He's sitting on the rocks, smoking, getting ready to dive in. A woman appears, walking down the path. Blond, a hat shading her face. He and Beth made love that first night, there on the rocks. They were married a few days later.

When they met, Beth resembled the island in its hateful phase, just as Libbie had resembled the lost island that belonged to another life. Beth and the island had been transformed at the same pace, her decay echoed the island's, as if one were feeding off the other. Her beauty had the same jaggedness that the landscape had taken on, and the landscape had the same light, subterranean and disordered, that played over her face. Mark worshipped Beth carnivorously, and through Beth he worshipped the island once more, carnivorously, and with the desire to tame it, to become its master.

With Beth he had really learned to drink. How lovingly, how patiently she taught him the secrets of alcohol!

And while he desired Beth's body and could never get enough of it, that same body also awoke other desires in him, ancient and forbidden. Perhaps it was her slim hips, or that boyish walk that made her seem so feminine, but slightly androgynous, too. He started to paint little boys. Boys walking home from school lost in thought, half-naked boys lying on sofas with a dreamy look in their eyes, boys' backs, hands, feet, noses, mouths—it became an obsession for him: all day, shut up in the house, he would paint that smooth skin, those young bodies, those innocent gazes. He forgot all about the island. He never painted nature anymore, not even as background. The boys were always in dark rooms, locked away, entirely his own. And he threw out all the bright colors. His boys lived in an endless night.

Confused images come to him. Beth stretched out naked on the bed, watching him paint a thigh.

Forget him. Come here. Don't you see how much I look like him?

Mark on top of her.

No. Make love to me the way you would to him.

Mark makes love to Beth while staring at the boy on the easel, who stares back at him.

He and Beth, drunk. Has it been days? Weeks? The house is littered with bottles and broken glass. He sees a piece slice through the sole of Beth's foot, sees Beth laughing, dancing, her blood flowing in torrents, the house turning bright red, the floor, the bed, the curtains, the walls.

Drink it! Beth orders, and Mark kneels and laps up the blood, licks her fingers—his pleasure, his sudden desire, the blood flowing from his mouth to hers and back again—then he licks her open eyes, tasting her eyeballs, and then the blood again, each of them sinking into the other's red, the room around them throbbing like a heart.

That day Beth conceived.

The hatred in her eyes as she watches her belly swell. The hatred in her eyes when she looks at Mark. Her awful cries and curses during labor. Her refusal to see the child.

Shein, four years old, is trying to open the fridge. How many days has it been since she ate? Beth is out. Mark, drunk, tries to help, but he can't even get a steady grip on the handle. Shein is scraping, pulling at the door with her little hands, but the fridge won't open. For the first time he sees hatred in Shein's eyes. Suddenly she looks like Beth.

Mark and Beth hit each other wildly, mercilessly. Shein watches through the window.

Shein, wearing Beth's hat, is out in the garden, mercilessly torturing a cat. Beth watches through the window, laughing.

Beth leaves with an Australian. That night, Mark, howling with pain, lights a fire in the yard and burns all the landscapes he painted when he was with Libbie. Shein watches the brushstrokes melt, the sea turning into nightmarish craters, the trees toppling, the skies bursting into flames.

Mommy, Mommy, Mommy! he hears Shein shouting into the fire. And then she screams *Fuck you!* and vanishes into the night. The search with flashlights and torches lasts until morning.

They found her on the same rocks where Mark had met Beth, and as he ran crying down the same path, it was as if the whole story were beginning again: the hat, the hidden face, the blond hair, the passion.

Only Shein's hair was full of blood and someone shouted, *Don't let him see her!*—and they covered her quickly with a sheet and Mark never saw her again.

Was it an accident? It must have been. How could Shein, so young, have known what suicide was?

"Bravo! You ate it all!"

Mark opened his eyes. Night was falling, the

moon was rising, and the island, shining, awaited his gaze. Mark thought that this must be what hell is like: to have the same beauty constantly before you so your eye can never rest on anything ugly or plain. To have lived entire lives, and yet have your gaze fall always on the same cliffs, the same sea, this eternal landscape that silently swallows loves, hates, unbearable pains, joys, and remains always the same, smooth and secret, something you're condemned to look at forever. Mark understood that this was the island's curse, and his punishment. Now the island hated him. Perhaps when he burned his landscapes the island had been hurt by the flames. And it took its revenge by taking Shein. But it still hated him—perhaps because their love had once been so complete that it still hadn't forgiven him for his betrayal. Mark saw hatred rising from the rocks, burning in the sun's rays, drifting over him with the scent of the sea. The island wanted to kill him, and it was killing him slowly and surely, day by day. How many lives had it given him? One, two, three, four? And now it was taking them all back, destroying them one by one.

And look at me now, back at the same café, at the same table, and everything's ended, not a trace remains, not a trace, nothing. The island has conquered me.

Emma came back with a stray dog in her arms. She was wearing her hat again, fished from the sea.

The café was empty. Sue, Gunther, Robin, and Mark looked at one another, suddenly sober, and quickly looked away again. When they were sober they hated one another, they would tear one another to pieces in a second, like wild beasts caught in the same trap. They rose, and the island rose around them, embraced them, gripped them, smothered them, protected them, adored them mercilessly.

14

"Give me your hand. The passage here is difficult."
Manolis was walking in front. They had been walking
since morning, now it was afternoon and they had
almost reached the top. The harbor below was
already cast in shadow, while the mountain still shone
golden in the sun. "I want to take you to a clearing no
one else knows about, a secret place. I want to see
you sitting on earth no one else has walked on. Sometimes when I sleep up there I see the sun sinking into
the sea at the exact moment the moon rises from
behind the mountain."

Luka's dress caught on a branch.

"Hold on." Manolis freed the fabric, then bent
and kissed it.

"I don't want you to do anything alone anymore.
I don't want you to sleep alone, write alone, comb
your hair alone, sit alone at a café. I want to become
your sleep, your blank page, the comb running
through your hair, the cup touching your lips, the
empty café where you sit in the morning." Manolis
scrambled up the rocks, turning at almost every other
step to look at her and talk to her. He was wearing a
loose white shirt. It was the first time Luka had seen
him in something other than his uniform. The shirt
billowed in the wind, Manolis laughed, his blond hair
shone. "Yes," said Luka, "yes, yes, yes."

"I'm scared, but it doesn't matter," Manolis said, tossing his head back and looking at the sky, laughing as if in defiance. "I thought maybe I should wait for some other love, but it would have been a mistake. There's no greater love than what I feel for you."

"I dreamed about you three times this winter. They were all nightmares," Luka said.

"What were you thinking about when you first came into my office?"

"The colors and patterns on a rug."

Luka was headed toward the ruins where the wells were.

"No," said Manolis hurriedly. "Not that way. The ground over there is dangerous, full of holes." Alan's body would still be there. The murder had taken place the previous day, and everyone still thought Alan had left on the hydrofoil. *No one would be looking for him anyhow*, Manolis thought, and felt sorry for him.

They reached the clearing. "Look," Manolis said, "look." The mountain was red and purple with poppies and anemones, the colors tumbled down to the sea, the rustling of leaves passed from tree to tree—the whole mountain was like a ship at full sail. Down on the waterfront, the churchbells rang out the hours, and for the first time all year they didn't sound mournful. The ringing bells now had an exultant air: the bells marked the passage of time, not its cessation, as they had in winter.

"Look at me," Manolis said.

Luka turned her head. Yes, his face was the face from her dream. "Your name is Emmanuel," she said suddenly. "That's your full name—that's what you were shouting in my dream, too, 'My name is Emmanuel,' only I couldn't hear."

With what devotion he took her face in his hands. With what devotion she rested her palm on his forehead.

Night fell. The wind died down. The moon's light was cold, metallic. The mountain, still and frozen, seemed dead; the white flowers were drained of blood; the trees had forgotten their connection to the earth and were stretching toward the sky as if in search of other roots.

Luka lay down. It was as if the stars had sunk low in the sky and were enveloping her in a strange warmth. She felt uneasy. It was a new, unfamiliar feeling, an expansion of the body, as if some wild animal were rushing through her, howling, filling her veins with mercury, and her blood thickened and slowed, until it was inching like a mass of stone toward her neck. *I'm dying*, she thought. *I'm dying, and will never have known Manolis's body.* And then, as if another thought were rising from her own body, *Perhaps that way I'll be spared something worse, something that's about to happen, something even worse than this beast that's choking me.*

Then she saw Manolis's face bending above her and her body became hers again, the sky went glassy, the evening star shone like the sun. Manolis covered her body with his, heart to heart, side to side, his naked legs pressed hers into the earth, and Luka clung to his neck, clutching his face to her chest. And although she lay there waiting, eyes closed, Manolis sat back up, rested his hands on the ground on either side of her face, and looked at her.

At that moment, for the first time, he saw himself lifting Kopesky and throwing him off the cliff. He saw the questioning look on Kopesky's face as he hung suspended for a split second above the abyss. He saw Kopesky's body falling slowly, landing face up on the rock, Kopesky still alive, smiling at him, watching him as he stood smoking at the edge of the cliff. He saw Alan kneeling and embracing the well, saw his butchered back, saw Alan smiling down at the waterfront for the last time. He saw himself going home and washing the knife, putting his hands under the faucet and watching the blood flow from his cupped palms. He saw himself lighting his first cigarette up among the ruins, blood under his nails, Alan before him, dead. He saw himself smoking calmly, staring down at the same illuminated waterfront that Alan had been looking at just minutes before he died.

And now he stared at Luka.

But how can I love her if I kill her? he thought. His hands stroked her neck. He rested his mouth on her hairline, which was slightly sweaty. He bit her lightly. He opened her legs with his own. His hands circled her neck. His head moved down her chest, he kissed her nipples through her dress. His thumbs met in the hollow at the base of her neck and closed. His hands gently squeezed her throat. Luka wound her legs around his waist. At the final moment, when he was about to sink his body into her flesh and his hands into her neck, he shuddered, rolled away, and plunged his arms up to his elbows in earth. "Don't come near me!" he shouted, holding his hands imprisoned in the earth. "Don't touch me!" he cried, pushing his hands even deeper, as if he were choking the dirt, as if the whole mountain were dying. He tried to thrust his whole body into the earth, to still his body with soil—he sunk his face in too, and his mouth filled with roots.

Luka wasn't scared. She felt such waves of love coming from the half-buried body beside her that she went over to him and rested her hand on the nape of his neck, as she might have done to a spooked horse. They stayed that way, motionless, Luka's hand heavy and sure on his neck, as the bells down at the port marked the passing hours.

Day was breaking as they headed back down the mountain. It was Sunday and the cantors in all the churches were chanting. High voices sung the glory of God all over the island, and all the bells rang. Manolis dropped Luka off in front of her house. She stared straight ahead at the sea, as if she were sleep-walking.

When he reached the harbor, Manolis went into the church and stood, as he did every day, in front of the icon of the Virgin. She looked like Luka. The same glad eyes in a sad face, the same mouth, thin and severe, the same vague smile. Was it a smile of promise, of love, or of cunning charm? Manolis bent and kissed her on the mouth. "I love you," he said.

Back at home he changed into his uniform, then left for the station. A few foreigners were sitting on the benches waiting for the police chief to renew their visas. The chief opened the door to his office and called, "Next!"

"Next," Manolis whispered. "Next, who will be next?"

That very morning, Luka went into the garden and dug up her pen. Not only was it not broken, but it worked perfectly, its ink thick and ready. Without worrying whether this was a miracle or a curse, whether she once again treasured the pen or still hated it, she laid it down in its old place beside her papers, closed all the shutters, and went to bed.

15

It was three in the afternoon.

The room was split into six different images, a still life in six stages of reproduction, one object looking at another and making it visible. Mina; her cats Coco and Shalimar sitting directly in front of her; the vase of daisies; the easel; the portrait of Manolis with the view from the window as a background; the view itself. When Manolis stopped outside the window exactly as he was in the portrait, the circle closed.

Mina looked down at her legs, her calves. They seemed so white to her, the flesh so vulnerable, so exposed, while Manolis's hands resting on the windowsill across the room were of difficult, silent flesh.

It was three in the afternoon and Manolis was standing at the window in his uniform. He looked just as he had when Mina had first seen him the previous summer when she'd gone to the station to renew her residence permit.

"How long can I stay?"

"As long as you like, if you'll paint my portrait," he'd said, laughing, as he stamped her passport.

She remembered that first day: there had been two gardenia blossoms taped to his telephone, on the three and the seven.

"It's my birthday today, I'm thirty-seven," Mina said. She looked at the gardenias, Manolis looked at her. At some point they both started laughing. She hadn't laughed in two years and it made her mouth hurt.

"I haven't laughed in two years."

"I know."

From that day on, she went to the station often. She would sit across from him, thin, silent, blowing her nose into a red handkerchief—she always had a cold and a slight fever. She never spoke, just watched as he made phone calls. The gardenias were fresh every day. Summer was over and she had no idea where he found gardenias in winter, but they were fresh every day, and always taped to the same numbers, the three and the seven. *He loves me*, Mina thought. When he made a call, he would crush the gardenias and they would give off a scent like night-flowers. Mina watched Manolis as he laughed, took down statements about rotten meat or dead dogs, talked with the officers who came in for a coffee. Mina just sat there in a corner, watching him, saying nothing.

Months later, she choked on a sentence and started to cough. She coughed all day long and that night when everyone else had gone home, she said, "Manolis," then stuck her hand down her throat and threw up. Manolis took the gardenias from the telephone and placed them in her palms, squeezed her

hands between his and looked at her. Mina understood that she would never be alone again.

"I was sick, very sick—I was depressed."

"You were sad," Manolis corrected her tenderly.
"Don't say 'depressed,' it's an empty word that means
an absence of pain." He was speaking to her for the
first time in the singular. He stroked a crease to the
left of her mouth. "The sadness shows here." He
stroked the crease and all of her pain concentrated in
that spot; his finger sunk into the crease and the pain
seemed to vanish and the crease became a scar.

"I was irresistibly drawn to chasms and gulfs, to
heights and depths, I wanted to jump off balconies,
roofs, boulders, mountains—I didn't want to die, I
only wanted to fall—and at night my dreams terrified
me. I would see bodies shooting into the air and
exploding, masses of flesh falling slowly into lakes of
dead water, and me sitting on the shore, knitting in
the rain."

As Mina spoke, people kept coming into the office
to file complaints, Manolis took down statements and
made calls. Mina spoke and the price of lamb mingled
with her dreams, the baker's illegal wall became her
height and her fall, and the days rolled by, and the
months, and the sickness faded as she listened to her
own voice, until one night Manolis stood up and
turned off the lights, and the sickness died.

That night in bed Mina felt cold. Now that it was
gone, she loved her sickness, she mourned its loss and

was scared without it. She hated Manolis for having taken it from her. She stopped going to the station. Every morning when she woke up she would say, "I'm fine," and her hatred for Manolis would grow. She was fine, and she didn't know what to do with this new monster of being fine. She missed her sickness. The sea was sweet and good on her body, bread tasted like bread, at night she dreamed of lions as she sunk into a sleep that smelled of nightflowers—but instead of being happy, she sought out the nightmares, the fear, the awful vitality of her sickness.

She started going to the station again. Now that she didn't love him anymore, she realized that Manolis was handsome. She put on makeup before she went, and sitting there would tug up her skirt and smoke one cigarette after another. And again there were statements, rotten meat and phone calls—but now there was something sharp in the air between them, something threatening. Sometimes his eyes watched her sadly. But most of the time he just looked at her painted lips with contempt. Then she would cross her legs higher and light another cigarette.

"The tomatoes were good today, the caique had just come in. I forgot to stop by the post office." Even phrases like these took on a cryptic, threatening air.

There was one gesture of Manolis's that haunted her. She saw it in her sleep, when she was shopping, as she walked, everywhere. Just imagining it was enough to make her blush, to make her palms start to sweat—it was, for her, unbearably erotic.

At the station: Manolis's hand lifts the receiver. His watch, low on his wrist, makes the gesture seem violent, precise. All day Mina stares at that hand. Later, that motion follows her everywhere, detached from Manolis. That endless gesture becomes more and more violent, faster, more rhythmic, like a nightmare taking on the automatic repetition of sex, the uncontrollable speed of a fall, the secret rhythm of pleasure.

Mina wanted that hand.

It was three in the afternoon. When Manolis stopped outside the window exactly as he was in the portrait, the circle closed.

Manolis looked at the house. All the houses on the island were charming, but this one had something sad about it, something abandoned, unfinished. It looked like Mina. Especially when you passed by and saw it from the road. Small, yellow, sunk into the rock, with a bitter laurel sprouting by the door, a plant that didn't grow anywhere else on the island. A sign posted out front read, *PROPERTY OF THE COUNTY*. A goat was rooting in the dirt for something to eat, but there was nothing there, not even brambles. The house was enclosed in an absolute silence, as if all the creeping and rustling of nature had forsaken it, as if not even the insects and birds could bear such sorrow.

When he came in, Manolis didn't sit in his chair to pose as he usually did, didn't straighten the crease in his uniform. Instead, he started to wander around the room, shifting the furniture and the books as if arranging the props for a play, dusting the tabletop with his sleeve, smoothing the bedspread, changing the water in the vase of daisies with motions that became more and more violent, more precise, as if he were covering the invisible tracks of an act that hadn't yet been committed. He pulled the curtains closed, and suddenly the room glowed red, as if the sun were radiating outward from this room, and everything smoldered like sources of light; the cats lay down at the head of the bed like two torches on an altar, one on the right, one on the left, and closed their eyes. Manolis pulled a piece of canvas over the stack of paintings on the floor, picking up one and placing it on the easel beside his portrait. It was a triptych Mina called *Daybreak, Noon, Dusk*, and it showed the island at those three moments. But in the red light of the room daybreak grew dark, noon was like night, dusk was like dawn.

"I want you to see me naked," Mina suddenly said. "Ever since that first day at the station when I sat and listened to the statements about rotten meat and dead dogs—I remember one woman whose dog had been poisoned, she kept saying 'King Charles Spaniel,' in English, and you didn't know how to spell it, and she kept crying and saying 'King Charles Spaniel,' and you wrote 'Sheepdog of unknown breed,' and that man who hung himself in his yard with a radio wire because his wife was always nagging him, and the souvlaki guy who sold plain pita with no souvlaki—ever since then I've wanted you to see me naked, your hand with the watch won't let me sleep, it strokes me tirelessly at night, it exhausts me—and the only thing you were thinking about was how to cure me, you looked at me and talked to me as if you believed you were Christ himself, and I watched how you lit your cigarette, how you answered the phone, I watched your mouth, your chest, your eyes—and now, when I paint, my fingers are yours, the view I see is the look in your eyes, my paint is your blood."

"But in the beginning…"

"In the beginning you always love the person who loves you."

"So what about you?" Manolis asked, his eyes full of sorrow and contempt. "What about you?" He looked at her. "Take off your clothes."

He took Mina's paints, the greens, yellows, blacks, purples, reds, dipped in the fingers of both hands, and began to stroke her entire body with color: her nipples green, her navel yellow, her eyes black, her pubic hair red—and there his hand slowed, he wanted that spot to be redder than red. Mina

swayed slowly over the hand that was filling her with
red fire, intoxicated by the smell of paint and turpentine and Manolis's cologne. Somewhere a churchbell
rang four times. Manolis took off his jacket and shirt
so he was naked from the waist up. He took his
revolver from its holster and stuck it inside his belt,
against his stomach. He stood before her, waiting.
Mina saw that his hands were no longer covered with
different colors, all of his fingers were now covered in
red, his hands were red up to the wrist. Mina
wrapped herself around him, her legs squeezed his
waist, Manolis bent, and together they fell onto the
canvas. When he entered her Mina felt the cold
metal of the revolver against her stomach. Manolis
was motionless, completely absorbed. Somewhere a
churchbell rang five, six, seven. Then Manolis drew
a red cross on her chest with his index finger. When
she saw the knife, Mina closed her eyes. Manolis
pressed its tip to the center of the cross, Mina arched
upward, and the knife sunk in to the hilt. It came out
and sunk in again, to the right, to the left, in the middle, up, down, again and again. "Look at me,"
Manolis said, "I want your eyes on me," as he stabbed
her mercilessly and the red paint and blood flowed
onto the canvas. Manolis's arms were red to the
elbows. Mina arched her body and let it fall, faster
and faster, more and more violently, rising to meet
Manolis's hand. An inexpressible pleasure filled her,
flooded her as she saw the blood spurting from her

chest, landing on the canvas, leaving strange shapes. Then she closed her eyes, and the last image that passed through her mind was of Manolis's hand with the watch low on his wrist, answering the telephone in the station: it's winter, it's raining, and that hand, the same hand that's about to kill her, lifts the receiver again and again, with the same violence and the same passion with which it now wields the knife.

Manolis rose and stood above her, his feet tight on either side of her waist. Then he took the bedspread and covered the body. He lit a cigarette, opened the curtains, and turned his portrait upside down on the easel so that the head was at the bottom. The churchbells rang ten. When he left the house the nightflowers had opened and a new moon was rising in the sky.

16

The sun was setting. The house filled with shadows, the paintings lost their glow. A last ray of light struck a thigh, a back. Darkness was falling fast. He didn't turn on any lights. The room smelled of turpentine. It was the time of day when Manolis usually came by. Mark would wash his brushes and clean up his paints as Manolis settled into a chair and smoked. They had gotten used to spending the end of the day together. Mark would wait impatiently for Manolis, to show him what he'd been working on. Sometimes in the afternoon he would stop in the middle of a painting because he needed Manolis to solve some problem of motion or color. Manolis never talked to him about art. He just looked at the painting. Then Mark would try to paint from within that gaze, to paint the way Manolis looked. Manolis's gaze had brought him to the verge of a major revelation, still unknown and mysterious. Mark felt that his work was acquiring its true proportions, reaching its apex, an apex that was inexplicably threatening.

He was waiting impatiently. He had just finished a painting. He went into the kitchen for ice and two glasses. When he came back, Manolis was standing in front of the easel.

"Pour me a drink. And turn on the spotlight."

"I just finished it."

"I can tell. The paint is still wet and you're all nerves."

Manolis smoked a entire cigarette while he examined the painting, then lit another.

"Well, what do you think?" Mark was impatient.

"I like it the best of all your headless boys."

"Why?"

"I don't know. Maybe because it's the most headless."

Mark laughed. "But none of the others have heads, either."

"Sure, but this one looks as if he never had a head, as if he'd already been decapitated when you painted him—I can't really explain it, but I see it."

Mark looked at the painting. His expression changed.

"You're right. It's the best boy I've ever done. And that's why."

Manolis looked at him thoughtfully.

"Don't let it bother you, the fact that you don't paint heads. Someday you'll be able to."

Mark laughed again.

"But I don't want to. It doesn't interest me."

"That's what I mean. Someday it will."

"You don't understand. A headless body is the most profound thing anyone could ever paint. And the most revolutionary. That's abstract art, the hard core stuff," Mark added in English. "My abstraction is real, I don't just distort things the way other artists do. My work is abstract because the most essential thing is always missing."

"Bullshit. Stop thinking and paint. And don't speak English to me. Have you ever painted heads?"

"Yes, but I left off the bodies."

They laughed so hard they couldn't stop.

Manolis went up to his portrait. "You painted me whole. Why?"

"I'll cut off your head later."

They drank, smoked, looked out at the night. A new moon was rising in the sky. The headless boys' had their bodies turned toward the window as if they wanted to escape. The portrait of Manolis watched them from a corner. The figure was raising a cigarette to his mouth, its tip glowing in the dark.

All they could see was the head. It looked as if it were floating, or sleepwalking, in search of its body.

17

Alfredo arrived on the island one afternoon on the last boat. He had a guitar slung over his right shoulder and was carrying a book, Cioran's *Précis de Décomposition*. He had come to stay with Placido. Placido and Ron had recently broken up, and Ron had sent Alfredo to him. They'd met in Zurich, and during their one and only night together, Ron had told him, "You should really go and stay with Placido, he's terribly lonely, and you'll love the island." Ron sent him without telling Placido, as a surprise, a kind of parting gift.

When Alfredo climbed down off the boat, he didn't look up even once to see where he was. He had a coffee at Antonio's, his face buried in his book. Then he went to the bakery to find out where Placido lived. Arhonto followed him to the door to make sure he actually left. "Christ and the Virgin Mary," she whispered. "What on earth was that?"

Placido was sitting on the terrace when Alfredo knocked on his door.

"Ron sent me," he said. "It's three hundred and fifty stairs up to your house. Do you have anything to drink?"

"No," said Placido. "And you're going straight to the hotel." He looked Alfredo up and down and found him ugly, strange. *Pity*, he thought. *If I wanted to screw him I'd keep him.* Then he reconsidered. *What the hell, I could use the company, and it might be interesting.*

So Alfredo settled in at Placido's house.

The next night Maggie invited them to dinner. Everyone had heard about the newcomer's arrival, and they were all curious to meet him. Alfredo and Placido arrived out of breath. "There are five hundred stairs to the front door, I counted," Alfredo said. He'd been there an entire day, and the only words he'd spoken had been about stairs.

It was the same group as always: Luka with Alana, who was much bigger now, Mark, Stanley and Boris. "This is Alfredo," Placido said.

They sat down at the table. Maggie had fixed a mystery vegetable and a strange meat dish that tasted like fish, and for dessert there were cookies and fruit sautéed in butter, brown sugar, and port.

Alfredo ate quickly and silently. He took several helpings of everything, and when dessert came he picked the brown sugar off the fruit with his steak knife and smeared it onto enormous slices of bread. *It's not that he's hungry,* Luka thought. *He's just eating because the food is in front of him. Like a camel filling itself with water before it crosses the desert.*

There's something lizard-like about him, thought Mark. *It's those narrow eyes and Slavic cheekbones, and that mouth, like a half-healed wound.* Mark felt nauseous and looked away.

That dirty ponytail... Placido was staring at Alfredo with an expression of disgust. *It's tied with a shoelace, of all things. Such unhealthy hair, so thin! Like an old woman's. If Stanley sleeps with him, he's nuts. Nice gift Ron sent me!*

Is he blond? Who could tell, under all that filth? Maybe... Luka thought of Manolis's blond head and smiled.

Stanley looked at Alfredo's body. *He's slim, but he's got no muscle. There's no way I'm screwing him,* he decided.

Alfredo pulled an exquisitely worked silver cigarette case from his pocket. As he lit his cigarette, they all noticed how beautiful his hands were.

Maybe it's because he's German, Mark thought. *Only the Germans can manage to combine vulgarity with that aristocratic air. He hasn't opened his mouth all night. But I'll make him talk.*

"How did you end up here?" He meant to ask in a friendly tone, but it came out sounding aggressive.

"I ended up on... on..."—Alfredo had apparently forgotten the island's name—"I ended up here completely by chance."

They all waited for something more. Nothing came.

"Marijuana brownies!" Alfredo suddenly cried, as if he had just woken up. They all stared at him, mouths hanging open. "Yes, yes, that's it, marijuana brownies! For hours I've been trying to figure out

143

what Maggie's dessert reminds me of. That's it, the recipe for marijuana brownies from Alice B. Toklas's recipe book, you know, Gertrude Stein's lover. Of course there's no marijuana, but maybe Toklas didn't use any either and just called them that for artistic purposes."

Mark felt the laughter rising in his throat, choking him. *Every day I sink even deeper into the insanity of this island. But tonight takes the cake...*

Then Alfredo began to speak without stopping, bulimically, the same way he had been eating. "Before I came here I lived for six months in a squat house, a bunch of us hippies and artists had taken over an abandoned factory, and no one could throw us out. It didn't have running water or toilets, we all slept on the floor and burned newspapers for heat, the painters did murals with scenes from the Bible. We were all going through a religious phase, though of course we wanted to express it in an avant-garde kind of a way—one guy painted God shopping at a supermarket, someone else painted a transvestite Adam, I wrote songs on my guitar based on the Gospels. Eventually the police came and shut the place down, it was infested with rats, though they didn't really bother us. Those were the most productive months of my life, your island is shit compared to that factory. There wasn't even a single window, it's how I'd always dreamed of living—here the houses are like ships, a porch here, a porch there, terraces on every roof, it's enough to drive you crazy. I hate nature, the smell of the sea makes me sick, looking at sunsets gives me cramps. I'm a man of interior spaces—I mean, would Kafka ever have written his *Metamorphosis* if he'd been smacked in the face with a view like that every morning? No, he'd have written *Heidi*, about the little girl who practically burst from all that milk up in the Swiss Alps, just like you guys are going to burst from all this beauty."

Even Mark, who was no longer surprised by anything, was flabbergasted. Alfredo stood up. "Placido, it's time we got going," he said in a commanding tone.

"Sorry, thank you, goodnight," Placido stammered, and they disappeared.

At home, once Placido had gone to bed and turned out the light, he felt a naked body slipping between the sheets. His disgust suddenly turned into an intense attraction, an arousal stronger than any he had ever felt before, stronger even than his first nights with Ron. *As if I were about to be kissed by a vampire*—that was his last thought before he closed his eyes and felt Alfredo's hot breath on the nape of his neck.

The next morning Alfredo had a headache.

"Too much fresh air," he complained. They were eating breakfast on the patio.

"Aren't you going to shower?" Placido asked.

"No. Water washes away the body's creative

juices. You should only bathe when you want to rest your mind."

Placido was in the shower for over an hour. When he came out, Alfredo was holding his guitar and there were pentagrams drawn all over the terrace.

"Do you want to hear one of my compositions?"

What Placido wanted more than anything was for Alfredo to take a shower, but he thought that if he were to expend his creative juices in playing the song, afterward he might want to rest his mind. "Yes," he said, "yes, I'd like that very much."

Alfredo closed his eyes, pounded his guitar three times with his hand, and let out a shriek. Placido's coffee cup shattered. Alfredo started to play, not with his fingers but with his fist, crashing it across the strings. His guitar seemed to be writhing in pain, emitting strange, unbearable sounds. At the same time, Alfredo screamed against the beat, shouting out numbers, and whenever he got to seven he would start over again. Then he jumped up and started running in circles around the terrace, smashing his guitar on the ground, jumping up and down on it, screaming louder and louder, until suddenly he dropped to his knees, kissed the tiles, spun his guitar around on his head seven times, and threw it off the terrace into the street. Placido had backed against the wall in terror.

"It's called *Revelation in D Major*," Alfredo said. "After John, of course," he added.

"You must have read the text very carefully…" Placido whispered. He was trying to find some way to make a run for the stairs, but Alfredo was blocking his path.

"Yes, of course, but I've gone beyond it. Too many monsters and trumpets for my taste, all sauce and no substance, like westerns, you know?"

"Yes, I agree," Placido said, though he was thinking, *This man is insane, and a complete jerk—how dare he talk that way about the most beautiful work of literature in the world!*

"If the end does come, it'll come some other way. From where you're least expecting it." Alfredo yawned, then winked at him slyly. "We've got some time, how about a siesta?"

Placido lunged for the door. "I'm going for a walk. There's food in the fridge. I might be late."

That evening as he was headed home, he could hear Alfredo's shrieks from far off. *Ron, why did you do this to me? Dear God, how can I keep him from playing his awful song on my terrace, in my house? I can't stand seeing my favorite text turned into that grotesque sight!* Placido went straight to bed.

The next day Alfredo had a headache again, a kind of tightening in his skull—"Like I'm wearing a helmet," he said, struggling to open his swollen eyes. Placido got the thermometer; Alfredo had a fever of 40° C. He kept asking for water. He tried to read the *Précis de Décomposition* but fell asleep with the book in his hand.

That evening Stanley stopped by. Placido left the two of them alone for a while, and when he came back, Alfredo was getting dressed and Stanley was lighting Alfredo's cigarette.

"Where are you going? You're burning up with that fever!"

"Stanley and I are going to the bar for a while. I'm going to stay at his place tonight."

"He needs some fresh air," Stanley murmured. Then Placido remembered that Boris was away.

The next afternoon Stanley had to carry Alfredo back to Placido's. "Quick! Call the doctor!" They got him to the bed, where Alfredo sat clutching his head in his hands, howling. "It hurts," he kept saying. "It hurts, it hurts."

Dr. Bournazis arrived, looked at Alfredo, and said, "Don't worry, it's probably just the flu." He pressed Alfredo's tongue down with a spoon to examine his throat, but didn't find anything. He listened to his heart. Nothing. He kneaded him all over. Nothing hurt. Then he sat down, lit a cigarette, and smoked in silence. After a while, he said, "I don't see anything wrong. Give him some antibiotics and if the fever doesn't fall by tomorrow, take him to the hospital for tests. It's not the flu or a cold or pneumonia, or any of the common viruses we have around here. Come to think of it, I don't like that fever one bit, combined with the pressure in the head. Those are symptoms of meningitis. Not a word to anyone—

it's very contagious, and can be deadly, and we don't want the islanders to start panicking. Like a helmet, eh?" he asked Alfredo.

"Yeah," said Alfredo, "yeah."

"And if it isn't meningitis?" Placido asked.

Dr. Bournazis looked at him uneasily. "I hadn't thought of that." He had been on his way out the door, but now he sat back down. He seemed uncomfortable, preoccupied. "Who is the patient staying with?"

"Him," Stanley quickly replied, pointing at Placido.

"Mr. Placido, is the patient a friend of yours?"

"Not exactly. A friend of a friend."

"What I mean to say is…" The doctor coughed, then stood up abruptly. "Well. I suggest you do a thorough cleaning of your house, top to bottom. Make sure the patient uses separate plates and glasses. You're to have no contact with him, understand, none. I'll stop by around this time tomorrow. In the meantime, I'll get in touch with the hospital. Goodbye, gentlemen."

"Nice gift Ron gave you," Stanley said when the doctor had left.

"Gave us, you mean." Placido smiled at him. Stanley left at a run, slamming the door behind him.

The next morning the pain and fever were so bad that Alfredo couldn't even open his eyes. They made their way to the hospital slowly, Placido's arm around Alfredo's waist. Alfredo, who couldn't see a thing, leaned his head on Placido's chest, his hair falling into Placido's face.

"The doctor said no contact," Placido said in desperation, "and here I am practically eating your ponytail!"

"The other night you liked it just fine. You kept asking for more."

Alfredo's voice was harsh. Placido felt ashamed.

The hospital was deserted, no nurses, no doctors, no patients. Placido set Alfredo down in a chair like a package, then went to sit on the other side of the enormous waiting room. They waited. The silence was absolute. There were religious pamphlets splayed out on little tables: *The End is Approaching!* and *Repent!* and *The Way*. Placido flipped through them absentmindedly. Alfredo leaned slowly to the left, a stupid smile on his lips as if he were seeing a vision. Time passed. A portrait of the hospital's benefactress hung on the wall. She was fat and bald, and glared at Placido angrily.

"She looks like Gertrude Stein," Placido said. Then he must have dozed off, because when he opened his eyes again, it was one in the afternoon. He heard footsteps approaching from far off. A nurse came down the stairs and walked over to him.

"Can I help you?" she asked in Greek.

Placido didn't understand. He pointed at Alfredo. "Sick," he said in English, "very sick." The nurse looked at Alfredo, who was at the far end of the room.

"Don't worry about him. You're first in line. Do you need to see a doctor?"

Placido started to shake his head frantically, pointing at Alfredo and speaking in broken Greek. "No me close! Me far! No touch. Sick!"

"Mairoula, come over here, this one's gone mad. Go call the doctor, tell him to come right away."

The other nurse shouted, "Doctor, doctor!" The doctor appeared out of the basement, a urine sample in his hand.

"Mairoula, this is from Father Yiorgos. We're testing for a urinary tract infection. He's coming for the results tomorrow before the morning service. What time does the church open?"

The nurses laughed. "How should we know? What is it, a boutique?" They glanced at him flirta-tiously.

"Come this way." The doctor looked at Placido. Placido looked at Alfredo.

"Him," he said.

"Excuse me?"

"I'm with him!" he howled, again in English.

"Calm down, don't shout, this is a hospital, we have patients here. If you're with him, why are you sitting so far away? Some phobia, a fear of hospitals? Mairoula, go get some Valium from my office, but discreetly, okay?" Then the doctor looked at Alfredo for the first time. He noticed his pale face, the swollen eyes, the dirty ponytail, the black nails.

"Okay," he said to Placido, "follow me."

His voice was cold. They went into his office.

"Are you a relative?"

"No."

"A friend?"

"No."

"What's wrong with the patient?"

"Phone Doctor Bournazis," Placido said, then added in Greek, "Bournazis knows."

The doctor made the call.

"Probable meningitis. Not a word to anyone. Mairoula, call the police. If the results are positive, we'll arrange with the chief for his deportation. I want urine, blood, everything, fast."

One of Placido's neighbors saw them as they were leaving the hospital. The day before, sitting out on her porch, she had heard Dr. Bournazis say the word meningitis, and now here the stranger was again, staggering, falling down the stairs. She crossed herself and went to tell her daughter-in-law, who ran to tell her niece, who told another aunt. By evening the whole island knew. The phone at the police station was ringing off the hook. "Send him away! Close the schools!"

Placido's neighbor became an instant celebrity; people kept calling to find out what she knew. "I'll let you know as soon as we have any developments." She turned off all the lights in her house, went out to sit on the porch, and waited.

But Alfredo didn't have meningitis, or any of the common viruses. All the tests came back negative. Placido's neighbor announced the results, and the islanders calmed down. Everyone but the doctors, that is, since Alfredo's fever raged on. There was talk of special tests that couldn't be done on the island. The foreigners didn't calm down, either. Fear spread like wildfire through their community.

Alfredo stayed in bed all day long with the shutters closed, because he couldn't bear the light. All he did was read his *Précis de Décomposition*, and when Placido, crying, begged him to go home and check into a hospital in Zurich, Alfredo answered: "No, this sickness is a kind of catharsis, and it chose this island to blossom."

"But it's blossoming in my house!" Placido cried, slamming Alfredo's door and heading down to the harbor at a run.

He started leaving the house almost at daybreak. In the beginning he would fix three meals each morning, then dash into Alfredo's room to leave them beside the bed. Later he started leaving only a glass of milk. The darkened room began to stink unbearably. Finally Placido stopped leaving even the milk. At night when he came home he would sit in a chair outside the closed door and keep watch—it seemed to him as if the sickness were lying in wait, ready to pounce if he so much as closed his eyes. One night he locked Alfredo's door and went to bed. The next morning he forgot to unlock it before he left. When he got back that evening he left it locked on purpose. He dragged a chair up to the locked door, sat down, and leaned his head against the wood.

"Go die in Zurich." His voice was almost tender.

The next morning he got a call from the station. Fortunately, it was Manolis.

"Your friend has to go. He's not wanted on the island."

"Manolis, you've got to help me, you've got to deport him. He's not my friend and he refuses to leave."

"By law, I can't deport him for an unknown illness. But I can help you."

"How?"

"Just don't feed him. He's in quarantine. If he goes out into the street, he's ours."

Placido laughed. "You'd think I knew. He hasn't eaten in days."

"No water, either. I'll call the town hall and have them cut you off. Then he'll have to go out."

"Manolis, what would we do without you?"

"You're asking me?" Manolis said, and laughed.

That afternoon Placido went to see Stanley. He was packing his suitcases, deathly pale.

"I'm going to the States, Boris is expecting me. I want to have the tests done there. Tell me... you and Alfredo..."

"Yes," Placido answered. "What about you?"

That evening Placido went to Bill's. As soon as he walked in he felt the atmosphere change. Behind the bar, Stephanos pretended not to see him. Utter silence fell.

"I'll have a gin and tonic."

Stephanos turned off the music.

"Get lost. I won't serve you."

Duane was there with two young guys, painters, recent arrivals. Without asking permission, Placido sat down at their table, lit a cigarette, and looked at Duane. "Hi, Duane. I know one of these guys. Very well, in fact. I won't tell you which, though, and I'm sure he won't, either. So, Duane, who are you going to take home tonight?"

Placido smoked his cigarette calmly, then got up and made the rounds of all the tables, sitting with everyone he knew, even with people he didn't. Soon there wasn't a single corner of the bar he hadn't touched, a single ashtray he hadn't used, a single arm he hadn't squeezed, a single glass he hadn't stroked. Late that night he ended up opposite Mark, who had been sitting alone in a corner and was so drunk he was painting in the air with amazing concentration, pulling his head back every now and then to get a better look at the piece. As soon as he saw Placido he raised his glass.

"To the health of our friend Alfredo, who came to this island to bring us this plague of the gods, so aristocratic, so refined, so exquisitely unknown—to our friend Alfredo, the new Marguerite Gautier, who instead of sniffing ether from a handkerchief reads the *Précis de Décomposition*, cultivating his mind to the bitter end. But times have changed, and sicknesses too, and... and... Hail, Alfredo, new symbol of romanticism!"

Alfredo was standing in the door. He had his hair down and it fell in waves to his shoulders. He had lost so much weight that his eyes weren't slits anymore, they were enormous, bright green, and his face had acquired a girlish delicacy. For the first time he was breathtakingly handsome. He was smiling, with a feverish glow. Barefoot, naked, wrapped in a blanket, he made a vague gesture with his hand that might have meant hello or goodbye. He went up to the bar and sat on a stool. He bent and put his mouth to Stephanos's ear. Those who were sitting nearby later said he had whispered, "Do you happen to have any German milk? The Greek kind seems watery to me, and Austrian milk doesn't agree with me." They all swore he had said exactly that, but no one believed them. How could someone so sick speak so lucidly about something so insignificant?

Mark started to laugh, but it turned into a sob as Manolis came in and took Alfredo gently by the shoulder. Alfredo leaned over and almost fell off the stool, and Manolis picked him up in his arms as if he were a baby and carried him outside.

The next day they learned that a boat had come during the night to take Alfredo away. Manolis had been the one to hand him over. Placido imagined Alfredo traveling through the night like the vampire Nosferatu, in a coffin on the deck of an empty boat that sailed crewless toward other shores, carrying with it—like Nosferatu—the plague.

A few days later Placido received a letter from Zurich:

> *Universitätsspital Zürich*
> *Departement für Innere Medizin*
> *Re: Herr Gublich Alfredo*

> We regret to inform you of the death of Herr Alfredo Gublich. He died on Tuesday at ten p.m. The analyses performed resulted in the conclusion that the patient, whose illness lasted from 22.2.84 to 12.3.84, had been infected with a certain contagion. It remained impossible, however, to determine the virus responsible.

> During his final hours, the patient wrote you a letter. He asked for it to be sent to you, along with the enclosed package.

Placido opened the package. It was Alfred's book, the *Précis de Décomposition*. A slip of paper fell from its pages. Placido picked it up and read:

"Then I took the little book from the angel's hand and swallowed it. It was as sweet as honey to the taste but when I had eaten it up it was bitter to my stomach." Dear Placido, by the time you get this book it will truly be "from the angel's hand," and the angel will be me. Read it. I doubt your insides will fill with bitterness, because I don't think you have any insides. A curse, then, from the afterlife— but with good intentions.

As always,

Alfredo

Placido threw the book and the letter into the sea. The words from Revelations started drifting into deeper waters. The *Précis de Décomposition* remained just where it had fallen, next to the pier. With each new wave it bumped against the rocks as if begging someone to fish it out of the water.

18

"Let me open the door. It's warped from the fire."

Manolis rolled up the sleeves of his uniform. Luka looked at his watch, the black band fastened low on his wrist, the veins that bulged as Manolis pushed at the burnt wood.

The house was high on the mountain, just above Mina's. It had burned down over the summer, along with the old man who had lived there, one night when the wind was strong. The old man was drunk and refused to leave, and as the flames closed in on him he started to sing "Life Has Two Doors." He locked his own door, then climbed into a cupboard, and when they put out the fire they found his skeleton holding a cup that seemed still to smell of retsina, his mouth hanging open in laughter as if he were still drunk. The house seemed haunted, shapeless and sad: ash fluttered everywhere through the air, falling from the ceiling like black snow. On the floor were fallen beams, charred mattresses. Perhaps that was why the view from the windows seemed so unique: it was the only thing that was still intact. It rushed from all sides into that ruined space, you could see the island from every point of view, another facet through each of the windows, as the island rose up, surrounding the house like a complex sculpture—and everywhere on the horizon, the sea.

Night was falling. They sat down on the floor. They gazed out at the island as it turned pink, then purple, then hung suspended in a faint, indefinable color until it fell, abandoning itself to some dark embrace.

"Whenever we're together, it's always night and we're always climbing to someplace high. I've come to associate you with effort and fatigue, it's as if my life is split in two."

"But the island is full of stairs, you're climbing all the time!" Manolis laughed.

"No, you don't understand. Whenever I go to see the others during the day, even when I go to Sue's, her house isn't any higher than mine. But with you I'm always climbing, and when you drop me off at my house, the strongest images in my mind are of endless stairs and the night and your back ahead of me as we scramble higher. I lie down, and from my bed I look at the mountaintops and the last of the houses and I want to get up again and start climbing, keep climbing until I reach that right angle where the island meets the sky. I feel as if you're there waiting for me. It's as if up there you become the island's unseen side, the face that's always in shadow. The whole island is secretive, but you're its darkest side, the last link in a chain of secrets. I often wonder what exactly you're hiding. Everyone on this island is hiding something."

Manolis didn't answer. He gave her a sweet look,

pulled her onto his lap, lit a cigarette for her from his own, and sighed.

"That clearing I took you to, lots of nights I go up and sleep there. I have the strangest dreams when I'm there, so beautiful that in the morning I wake up feeling completely refreshed, and all around me nature exudes this strange warmth. Once when I got there I even felt as if the trees and the soil recognized me, remembered me, had been waiting for me impatiently. That was the day the dreams began."

"You only have them when you're there?"

"Yes. That's why I like high places now, and night. I've come to associate altitude and darkness with a kind of tenderness—it's a time when I let my mind wander, when I dream, when my cigarette seems to taste different. It's the time when I love you."

"You mean you don't love me the rest of the time?"

He looked at her. "I save you for the night."

They smoked, gazing out at the view. Mina's house was directly below them. Empty, silent, a padlock on the yellow door, uneven black letters scrawled over the right side of the wall: *FOR SALE.* Manolis looked at the house, his cigarette dangling from his mouth, his eyes half closed in the smoke.

"Did you know her?"

"Yes."

An overwhelming, irrational jealousy swelled up in her.

"Did you know her well?"

"As well as anyone could know Mina."

Luka looked at his profile: the cigarette, the half-closed eyes fixed on the yellow door with an odd look of absorption, concentration. *It's natural for him to stare like that*, she thought. *After all, he saw the corpse. Who knows what he's remembering now. And whom he suspects of committing the murders.*

"Did you write anything today?" Manolis always asked her that, a bit ironically, but tenderly too, with a kind of secret admiration.

Luka laughed. "Every day everyone asks me if I wrote. Half of them are happy if I say yes, the other half if I say no. That's how I know who loves me, I can't imagine a better way of separating my friends from my enemies. Though sometimes things get confused. Like with Anezoula: she loves me, perhaps more than anyone, but she's happy when I don't write, she wants me to be sad. Maybe then I give better massages."

"And maybe you love me more on the days when you don't write!"

They smiled, close again, accomplices.

"Do you dream, Luka?"

"Yes." Luka thought of her dream with the piglet, and the name Manolis. She would never tell him about that. "Tell me about some dream you have all the time," she asked him. "We all have a recurring dream, sometimes the same one since childhood.

Describe yours to me."

She rested her head in his lap. He ran his fingers through her hair, spread it out in a fan around her face, stroking it, smoothing it over his pants, tender and absentminded, close to her, yet somewhere else entirely.

"You pet me the way I pet Alana!"

Manolis laughed. "It must mean I love you." He lit a cigarette and squinted again. "Ever since I was a kid I've had a dream that scares me. Every time, while I'm sleeping, I think that if the dream changes or ends in some other way, it'll mean I've changed, too—and as soon as I wake up, I feel like I have to go back over the dream, to study all its details and compare the changes in the dream with the ones in real life.

"I dream that I'm walking on a beach. The sea is completely still, black and thick and sulfurous, the pebbles hot and sharp under my feet, the sky dark but cloudless, as if night were falling suddenly, though it's the middle of the day. Beneath this suffocating stillness I feel the earth—deep in its bowels—preparing for some change. That's why it's so still, it's gathering energy. The water swirls around my naked feet, burning hot. It doesn't caress them in its usual gentle way. It slaps at them nervously, as if even the sea had lost its rhythm. That's what scares me the most: it's as if nature were suffering some kind of palpitation, a panic, something that keeps halting its pulse, then the next moment makes it beat madly, wildly.

"And then I see it: a tidal wave rising up before me. Silent and monstrous, the foam at its crest touching the sky, it moves toward me like a snow-capped mountain, doubling over to gather speed, advancing slowly, solemnly, headed straight at me. No matter where I hide, I can't escape. I start to run. I fall, then get up again, I'm crying and running like a madman, the wave is still far away, but that frightens me even more: its slow rhythm, its awesome majesty as it approaches without the slightest need to hurry. I always associated fear with some sudden conflict, death with some quick movement that catches you unaware. And here I am, watching as my death approaches so slowly it seems not to be moving at all. But I know that at some point it will reach me, cover me, shatter me with an inhuman power, a nameless, faceless force, pulled up from the hot depths of the sea—and it's funny, because ever since I was a kid the only thing I've been scared of is diving, disappearing under the water. My fear grows so intense that it's no longer an emotion but a cosmic fear, an element of nature, like the wave itself.

"Now I can hear the water rushing, an unearthly sound that rises into the sky like a song. It seems as if I'm hearing children's voices, high, complex harmonies. The wave is approaching. I'm running alongside it. From this close I can see the bulge in the middle, like the guts of some huge sea monster. I look at the crest: it's moving with dizzying speed, sucking in air, though the base of the wave stays motionless, as if churning in the depths of the sea. I fall down again, my head hits a rock, my mouth fills with seaweed, I feel dizzy. I see a crab clinging to the bottom of a rock, trying, like me, to hide. Now the wave is blocking the whole horizon, everything around me is completely dark. I want to get up but I can't, an irresistible force, an attraction holds me stretched out on the ground, paralyzed, given over to the monster that's approaching. The rushing noise becomes a groan, the wave is almost touching me, I can feel its cold, wet breath on my back—and then at the last moment I stand up, stretch my hands toward the sky, sink my feet into the sand, and stand there waiting. I rise up before it, I don't want it to find me weak, lying down. Now I'm practically inside the wave, I can see it in detail, the color at its crest, a blinding sea green that gets darker further down, all the way down to its inky base. Spatterings of color everywhere, red, yellow, gold... Faced with such absolute beauty, my fear evaporates, this death doesn't scare me anymore, because it's bigger than anything I've ever known, I'm about to be absorbed into some divine vision, to become part of a kind of cosmogony, and I'm quivering with love and impatience—*It chose me*, I think, *I'm the only person the wave is going to swallow. Just as Jonah entered the belly of the whale, this wave will take me inside it. Me, only me.* And so I embrace it, I accept it, I offer myself up to this wave that rushes over me, groaning, and my last thought is, *I've been saved."*

Manolis bent over Luka, staring at her. The hand holding his cigarette was shaking.

"Luka, what does that dream mean? It scares me. There are things I've done in my life that I want so badly to tell you about, Luka, things I don't understand, like the dream—and they're unbearable."

"Don't tell me about them, I prefer your dreams. They make it easier for me to approach the things you've done. Because your dream becomes mine, too, while a real moment from your life, a movement, a gaze, will always remain a mystery to me, something I can never know, unless I'm there to experience it. But dreams are common property, they circulate in our blood, we can share them, trade them."

"Sometimes," Manolis said, "I feel like this whole island is a dream, and each of us has a place, a role, and no matter how hard we try to understand what it means, we can't, because we're part of it, maybe even the protagonists. Or maybe we're like sleepwalkers pacing an island that doesn't exist, dreaming an island that doesn't exist, all dreaming the same dream at the same time. Sometimes in the morning on my way to the station as I light my first cigarette of the day, the harbor before me still sunk in darkness, I have such a feeling of nonexistence that I sit down on a step by the sea and close my eyes. I'm scared that when I open them the island will have disappeared. Other times I feel like I'm at the center of a dream that lights up the world and guides it. I feel like the island is that dream, and I'm the one dreaming it."

"It's strange," Luka said. "Our dreams resemble one another, but they're opposites. Both of us dream about the sea, but yours tries to drown you while mine pulls away from me. Though how could we not dream of the sea when it surrounds us on all sides?"

"In my dream, I'm sitting high up on a rock. Down at my feet the sea glistens. It's summer, I'm hot and thirsty, I've been sitting on this rock for days, my skin and mouth are dry, if I don't get to the water soon I'll die. I scramble down and run until my feet are almost touching the first wave. I watch as the sea pulls away. I run and run, but the water keeps receding, so I run faster, and the water draws back faster than I can run. The landscape is rocky, and I have to keep scrambling up and over these enormous boulders. *Now*, I think, *when I reach the top of this one the sea will be there, directly beneath me, and I'll dive in, I'll be saved.* But when I look down I see the water pulling back with frightening speed. From the next rock the sea is nowhere in sight. The landscape changes, taking on the dry, inhuman glow of the desert, nothing but rocks and sand stretching to the horizon. My skin cracks, it's covered with wounds, my tongue swells, the sun pounds down on me mercilessly. I fall to my knees and cry inconsolably. I look at my body. There are huge, deep wrinkles all over it, like whip marks. In just a few minutes I've grown old."

As in her dream, Luka was crying inconsolably, the way children cry when they're hurt but don't know where. She clung to Manolis's neck and he hugged her, rocked her. "Cry," he said, "cry."

"How can I write when I'm afraid of pain and old age, when I'm afraid of everything?" Luka said through her sobs. "Would you love me if I were covered in wounds, like in my dream? Would you love me if I had leprosy, if I were disgusting, if I were old? Ever since I was little that's how I've measured love, I think, *No really one loves me for myself*, though I have no idea what that means. And would I love you if you were ugly, if you were sick would I kiss your wounds? There's a child hiding inside of me, her eyes squeezed shut in fear, and an old woman, her eyes wide open in terror. I know them both. It's Luka I don't know."

"The things you're saying touch something deep inside me. Talk to me, keep talking."

"When I was little, I would sneak next door to see the old man who lived there. His room smelled the way rooms smell where people are dying, a mixture of mildew and damp. I adored that old man. He always sat in an armchair by the window and the light fell onto his hands, his dry skin, and each day the light showed more and more blindingly how death was touching those hands the same way the hands touched the arms of his chair: he would grip the chair more and more tightly each day, he didn't want to leave. I would kneel and kiss his hands with such love, such passion, something I've never felt for anyone else, not even you. I would kiss his palms, and I remember they were so dry they left my mouth red and chafed. I started telling him stories full of water, springs, rivers, torrential downpours. I made them up on the spot, so they were disjointed, surprising, crazy, but the old man would listen and smile. Perhaps he would have died sooner if my stories hadn't drenched him in that cool wet relief. I would describe a sudden rain falling on some city, how the sidewalks shone, and the roofs, how people in the streets ran for shelter as the first streetlights flickered on. Then his hands would relax and let go of the arms of the chair for a while. 'Luka dear, tell me another,' he would say. It was in that room, with that dying old man, that I learned to write. If my stories had the power to keep death at bay, to quench a thirst, to fill the room with presences more alive than the lamp, the bed, the dirty glass, then they had the power to actually change the world. Ever since, I've tried to write the way I used to talk to that old man. But I don't have that flame anymore, that love. The old man was my first reader. And my last."

"I feel that same compassion, when faced with death, with the end, it's a feeling more passionate than love. I didn't know that you, too, I never imagined… Luka, I've done things that are as inexplicable as dreams."

"We all have."

"If you ever find out what I've done, remember your story about the old man. Maybe you'll understand."

"Tell me about a woman you've loved."

Manolis laughed. "Before you came along or now?"

"Now," Luka said, laughing too.

"As soon as I step into the church, I can feel her waiting. It's dark, my eyes have to adjust. In those few seconds before I see her, such a fever, such an enormous passion swells inside me that my legs start to shake and I have to lean against one of the standing pews. Her face lights up slowly, revealing itself only to me—I've never seen a face undress itself like that, no nakedness can compare with hers. She offers me first her forehead, then her cheeks, then her mouth, and with such abandon, such knowledge of love that when I finally see her face the pleasure is almost unbearable, I close my eyes. Blind, I've approached her without realizing it. I count her eyelashes, lose myself in a beauty mark to the right of her mouth, imagine the breasts beneath the thin fabric. I want her. I want to curl up in her arms like a child, to lie on her like a lover, to kneel down and worship her, to push her to the ground and cover her with kisses, to wound her in her most private places. From the way she looks at me I know she feels it, too: my mother and my lover, virgin and whore, I've made her a woman. It drives me mad, this double game in which she hides her face and mouth with a mother's severity but the mating call of the female. I want her. I move even closer, rest my hands on the glass, bend down as if to plunge my whole self into her. My body presses wildly against hers, my kiss is deep, endless, I feel her lips open, and the act of love is completed, there in the dark of the church. Beside her icon is a basil plant in a golden pot. One day, at the height of my passion, I knocked it over with my hand, and when it fell the whole church seemed to shake, the saints in the frescoes seemed to close their eyes. That basil plant always gives the moment a heavenly fragrance, a sweet smell of infinity. I've never loved a woman like that."

"But you love her more than you love me."

Suddenly all love drained from the room, the magic had vanished. It was just a charred, abandoned room again, a strange, hostile place.

"I have to go." Manolis stood up.

He's going to the church to see her. She's waiting for him.

For no reason, Luka suddenly thought of the murders. Kopesky, Alan, Mina. She remembered Anezoula's descriptions during their massage sessions: the butchered corpses, the knife wounds, Mina's naked body covered in so much blood that it had stuck to the canvas, Alan's hands twined so tightly around the well that no one could pull them off. Anezoula told her that Manolis had been the one who finally managed to pry them loose. Anezoula was very fond of Manolis. "You should go out with him, Luka," she always said, "he's so handsome, and a policeman, too." Manolis had never spoken to Luka about the murders, but that was natural, since they never talked about his work. She looked at him. He was standing in front of the window, the island springing up behind him. His face was in shadows, his body only visible from the neck down, just as in Mark's painting before he had finished it: headless, a stranger.

Who is he? Luka thought, and for the first time she felt scared. *Who is this man who dreams about tidal waves, who makes love to the Virgin but never touches me, who seems more distant than a passerby on the street yet more familiar to me than myself?*

Manolis left without looking back, without saying goodnight.

He's punishing me for not being some unapproachable, smiling icon behind glass. He wants me to be incorporeal, divine.

But she sensed something else, too: there was another reason for this denial of the flesh. Some prohibition. As if for Manolis flesh were inextricably linked to an act of violence, maybe something fatal. Her mind, an insect moving through the dark, encountered something unbelievably monstrous, was frightened and went the other way. The momentary insight left her weak, as if she had looked down from a great height. She felt a vertigo, a dreadful anxiety. *Who is he?* She was alone in the burned-out ruin. On the slope below she could see Mina's house, the padlocked shutters, the donkey, the bitter laurel, the sign that read *PROPERTY OF THE COUNTY.* Luka rested her head on the charred windowsill and fell asleep. Again, she dreamed her dream. She was running along the shore, trying frantically but in vain to reach the sea.

19

Luka got up, made coffee, sat down at her desk, and pushed away the reams of paper, keeping only a single white sheet before her. She uncapped her pen. For the first time in years she didn't tell herself she had to write. She didn't even think about the fact that she was writing. She didn't feel moved, or inspired, or afraid. But the text itself throbbed with emotion, inspiration, fear. After the tenth page she stopped and read what she had written. It was the first chapter of her novel. That afternoon she went for a long walk. Inside her pocket her hand was still writing. She thought of Manolis. Now that the ink flowed through her veins again with an exhilirating momentum, now that she no longer had any need of love, now she could have loved him. She felt him, too, flowing through her veins, frightening and familiar, like the book. But just as the book had rejected her for so long, now he too was pulling away, like the sea in her dream. *He too has something to finish.* Luka was walking on the path above the sea. She leaned over the edge of the cliff. The rocks below were black, sharp. *There isn't much time, I have to hurry,* she thought, not knowing if it was the book she was thinking of, or the fact that it was getting dark and she had to get home because she had forgotten her flashlight.

20

"You understand, Manolis," said the Chief. "I'm a homosexual. I don't hide it, but I'm careful. I'm an art lover, too. I'm naturally polite and would never take advantage of my position, I just let it be understood. You know what I'm getting at."

"Sure, Chief."

"I knew you would, you're a modern man. I see you spending time with the foreigners, you've almost become part of their community, and I know how hard that is, it's not easy to break into their circle." He thought for a minute. "Maybe it's because you're blond. You do look kind of foreign. The first time I saw you I thought you were Norwegian."

"Come on, Norwegian?" Manolis laughed.

"Swedish, then. Something northern, anyway."

With the word "northern," the Chief's mouth went slack, he ran his tongue over his lips as if eating a piece of Turkish delight. "Oh, those northerners with their blue eyes and big, beautiful bodies! They're such idiots, though, and they're obsessed with the temperature. 'In Oslo it gets down to thirty below, Celsius,' they tell me. 'That's incredible!' I answer, melting. 'And in Copenhagen? Does it ever hit negative forty?' I don't give a shit about the temperature, but it drives me wild to hear them speaking Swedish or Norwegian, all those *ü*s, it's pure poetry, all those velvety, songlike sounds, their round, wet lips like little buds—I'm telling you, Manolis, I could faint. Then again, there they are talking to you like overgrown babies, like enormous cows, and at the same time they're downing bottles of vodka like it's water, their blue eyes go blurry and they start to get aggressive. A strange bunch, those northerners! But the worst thing isn't the alcohol. It's that, fuck it, they're straight." The last word was in English.

"What's that, Chief?"

"Straight, Manolis. They're not into it, they don't do it, you know? They only dig women. That's my problem: all the guys I like are straight. They're the only ones who turn me on. I don't like fairies at all, I like real men."

"What am I?" Manolis asked, smiling.

"As straight as they get!"

"Where did you learn that word, anyway?"

"A friend of Placido's came down to the station for a residence permit. I was coming onto him, but discreetly, I told him about my village, about the Acropolis, how the ancient Greeks weren't just great at philosophy, they were all homosexuals, too. He was a friend of Placido's, how was I supposed to know... And he laughed, I remember, and said that he'd studied philosophy in Copenhagen, but that he was straight. Oh, Manolis, this island is a whorehouse, that's why I like it. A classy one, though. Just imagine if I'd been sent to Tripoli! When they transferred me here, I was thrilled, I felt like I was headed to Europe, to Venice. Doesn't the island remind you of Venice? The narrow streets, the old Italian mansions—after all, the Venetians built half the island. And all the foreigners living here give it an international flair, don't you think? It's an odd place. Even you're kind of different. I do my job right, though, I don't let anything get in the way of that. But you know, ever since I was a kid I had a thing for foreigners, and now here I am, Chief of Police in this Tower of Babel. I even smoke Dunhills, they seem like the most foreign cigarettes, I don't know why, maybe it's the box. I even bought a red lighter to match. What do you smoke?"

"Camels."

"See, you smoke foreign cigarettes, too. Only yours are strong, for cowboys in Arizona. Dunhills are aristocratic."

"Chief, for a long time I've been wanting to tell you how pleased I am to be working with you. We both like foreigners, we have the same tastes...."

"Except in one thing, right?"

They both laughed.

"Tell me, Manolis, haven't you ever... Weren't you ever curious, you know, to see what it's like? Hasn't anyone ever caught your eye? I bet a million guys have come onto you, you're such a doll. You look northern but you're Greek, there's no more tantalizing cocktail. Don't take this the wrong way, but you're every homosexual's dream."

"But Chief, I'm straight!"

They laughed, smoked, drank coffee, the bells down at the port rang ten, sunlight drenched the office, the German shepherd chained up by the door barked, and the caique, the *Agia Eleni*, was unloading furniture for the sheikh's house, all of it gold: beds, nightstands, statues, carvings, domes with golden angels, fountains, tiles of precious stone, a bathtub, also gold, rare plants from Africa—it was all tossed in the middle of the port beside supermarket crates full of toilet paper, bleach, butter and cheese, Azax for the windows, Baygon for the roaches. Even down at the station they could hear the men shouting:

"Hey Vassilis! Watch the tub! Tie it sideways across the mule so it doesn't fall off going up the stairs. Just think, taking a bath in two tons of gold. I'd be so scared of scratching it I'd just sit there like a mummy."

"Man, what do you care? We're getting twenty thousand drachmas for every trip we make. Two more palm trees and the angel's gold dick that broke off in the crossing and I'll be able to go to Yiorgos's tonight and buy a color TV. I wish I had a gold dick, the chicks would come running when I whipped it out. The sheikh must have one just like it, that's why he goes around like he's shit in his pants, that's how heavy it is."

Everyone down on the dock laughed. Manolis and the police chief had gone to the window and were leaning out, laughing along, smoking and looking out at their island.

"Is there another station like this in the world, Manolis? Where a police chief could talk the way I'm talking to you now? Every Friday I watch this show on TV, *Hill Street Blues.* Check it out sometime. It's the perfect police station, from the interior decoration to the officers' conduct. The chief is a Chinese guy, kind of a sissy, he's always guzzling coffee and doesn't speak a word of English, but nobody cares. That's freedom! That's New York for you! Everyone's coming and going, smoking, drinking coffee, and the suspects, the criminals, the addicts, they're all dressed to the nines, and the officers practically apologize for having caught a guy with two kilos of heroin. That's civilization. Here you're lucky if we don't beat you up for bringing in a wallet you found on the street. And you wouldn't believe how the place looks, plants and paintings everywhere. I've set myself a goal: I'm going to fix up our station real nice, make it gorgeous, just like the one on *Hill Street Blues.* Here we've got calendars with pictures of beaches plastered all over the walls, they make me want to throw up. I'm an art lover, you know, a collector. I've been collecting paintings for a long time. I mean, the island is crawling with painters. And I found the perfect trick, so they don't just give me their paintings for free, they even paint me whatever I want."

"How, Chief? That's incredible!" Manolis was enjoying himself. He loved the chief and sometimes felt sorry for him. The chief liked to think he was sophisticated, but he was really so innocent.

"Okay, listen to this, it's ingenious: when they come to ask me to renew their residence permits and for whatever reason they're not legally allowed to stay, I tell them, 'Look, if you do this painting for me, I'll give you a renewal, not just for three months, but for a whole year, okay?' They go nuts. 'But,' I tell them, 'I want a special painting, I'll tell you exactly what I want.' So there you have it. At this very moment, all the painters on the island are working for me, it's like I'm some kind of patron of the arts. They wouldn't work that hard for the sheikh himself! Jane is doing an abstract piece, I'm going to hang it in the hall. 'Pollock style,' she told me—I don't know the guy, but he's a foreigner, so he must be good. Duane is doing a painting of my office, Placido the front of the station, and of course I asked Mark to do my portrait. I'll hang it over my desk. I'll be reading *Newsweek* and smoking a Dunhill. Too bad Mina died. I was going to ask her for a sunset, it was her specialty. Or else she was going to paint Tony, standing next to my bed. Speaking of Mina, we need to talk about the murders, but later, this is more important. Of course none of it's exactly legal, but then, who's to know? Once I've got my hands on all the paintings, what do you say, should we have an

180

opening? We'll be the only ones on the island with that kind of collection!" The police chief sighed. "Oh, Manolis! This isn't a police station, it's a garden, a paradise!"

He lit a Dunhill.

"Do you play poker?"

"No."

"You should. I'll teach you. I play, but you know what I do? Betting is against the law, so no one ever takes money from me, since they know that if they do, I'll report them. Get it? So when I win, I pocket the money. When I lose, I don't pay anything. That's kind of illegal, too, but again, who's to know?"

"Who's Tony, chief?"

"Tony, Manolis, was the great, the only love of my life. A hairdresser from New York, a real doll. He even used to cut my hair. I adored him. I had set him up in my house, though of course I kept quiet about it. What can I say? Ours was an insane passion, a homosexual Harlequin romance, *Him and Him*. But I lost him, my Tony. One of the locals stole him from me, that kid with the yellow caique. One night Tony came over, we'd just split up and I was hoping for some kind of explanation, and then Homer—that's the kid's name—shows up and starts pounding on me, beats me black and blue, then grabs Tony and they leave. Homer only wanted him for his money. What do you think, that the islanders are saints, that the only ones having orgies around here are the foreigners? The locals are the worst of all, because they do it for the money. They ask for jewelry, gold watches, chains. Whole houses have been built with the money of foreign fags. The men here only do it for the money, I'm telling you. The foreigners do it for fun, but the islanders are completely corrupt, it's all about self-interest. They don't really like it, they're straight, they just screw the guys and pocket the money, and then they get married, build a house, buy a TV. All those married men you see, and the single ones too, the ones with mules and caiques, they're all ruining the market for the rest of us. Anyway, that's how I lost my Tony—and see how long my hair is these days? I don't have the heart to let anyone else cut it."

The police chief's eyes had filled with tears. He pulled a pink handkerchief out of his pocket, wiped his eyes, and popped a mint in his mouth.

"Let's talk about something else. What do you say, Manolis, should we talk about work for a while? What do you think of these murders? What with all this drama in my personal life, I haven't had much time to get involved. Have you come up with anything? Do you have anyone in mind?"

"Not yet, Chief."

"Terrible situation. That kind of thing would go unnoticed in New York, but this is a small place. Such brutality! Did you see the bodies? I almost fainted. Who could butcher a human body like that? Who could stab a person so many times, with such fury, such madness—did you see Alan's back, Mina's chest? I know the foreigners and I know the locals, and none of them could commit such heinous crimes. Of course, someone did. But who?"

"Maybe someone who was just passing through."

"Get busy on this one, Manolis. You've got to help me. If I don't solve these crimes, they'll transfer me. And it would kill me to have to leave."

Shortly afterward, the police chief was transferred. They sent him to Tripoli. The foreigners threw a goodbye party for him at Bill's bar. The chief got drunk and cried the whole night, making toast after toast. Toward the end of the party Bill opened a bottle of champagne, stood up on a table, and gave an incredibly long toast in lots of different languages; he even threw in some Greek. The police chief kept saying "I love you" to everyone, in English, and crying uncontrollably.

The new chief would be arriving soon. He was rumored to be a tough nut, and had sworn to catch the murderer in a matter of days.

21

At the station, the new chief was drinking milk and putting his papers in order. "Evaporated milk is better than the fresh stuff," he said.

Manolis was sitting across from him, smoking.

"Why don't you quit?" said the chief. "I did, to set an example. What do you need them for, anyway? It's just another weakness. When I'm sitting here, I don't want the guy standing on the other side of my desk thinking, 'He's a smoker, too, I'll outsmart him somehow.' I want to be perfect, understand? No neuroses. I've quit everything. That's how I got to be chief. All I think about is my work. A cup of coffee in the morning and that's it. And we've got real work here, not fun and games. What's your take on the murders?"

"There've been a lot."

"That's all you have to say? Unbelievable. So many murders and nobody seems to care. As if it's totally normal. I've never seen anything like it. No one's looking for evidence, no one's worried. But we have a responsibility to the victims. I don't know where this one will lead me, but I'll find him. I can smell him. He's still on the island, right under our noses. He's getting ready for some new trick, working himself up again, little by little. I can almost see him. And yet for the first time in my career I can't tell what kind of person he is. He's evidently insane. But if so, how can he circulate so freely among us? And where did he learn to kill with such skill? Is he queer? After all, he raped Alan. But he raped Mina, too. These things are beyond me. A fag, a cocksucker, a lady's man, a sex fiend, a murderer—what can I say, I've never seen anything like it. There isn't a single case like it in any of my criminology books. You're this, you're that, or you're the other thing. It's a bad situation, Manolis. This island is completely perverted. How could it not have a murderer like this? You see a girl down by the dock—'Look at that chick,' you think, and she turns out to be a boy. You see some boy from behind with a back like an ox, he turns around, he's got tits out to here. How am I supposed to make sense of it all? I was brought up with morals. At any rate, I've got one thing figured out: the murderer is a foreigner. No Greek could be that perverted. Sure, we've got our weaknesses. If he were just a fag, I'd be looking at the Greek side of things, too. But playing for both teams—sexually, I mean—that's just too much. Even the Greek fag has morals. They may be messed-up morals, but even he's a family man, in his way. Only a foreigner could be a little bit of everything. It's how they've been raised. I heard that in Sweden the whole family takes baths together, all of them naked, parents, kids. So how could the poor things not end up a little confused?"

The police chief's voice seemed distant to Manolis, almost melodic. He looked out the window. The island was unrecognizable. He'd been feeling strange for a while. Now his body started to burn, every vein in his head was pounding, and an intense pressure around his heart made it hard to breathe. Something terrible was coming, something uncontrollable. Unknown, unnamable. He had to hide. He stood up and heard his chair fall to the floor behind him, the chief shouting something after him as he ran down the stairs. He crossed the waterfront doubled over, hands clutching his stomach as if he were in unbearable pain, his body swelling, about to burst in the air like the effigy of Judas that they fill with dynamite at the stadium on Easter Monday and shoot at until it explodes.

"Hide, I have to hide," he kept repeating. He ran blindly toward the mountain, careening into doorways in the narrow streets, not raising his eyes, crying as he ran toward his hiding place. When he reached the clearing, he fell to the ground and threw up. The earth drank in his vomit. He threw up again and again. The soil steamed. He had seen all this before, had lived it before—that was his final thought. Then he grew calm. He felt drained of all emotion, good or bad, and the serenity that filled him was cold. It started to rain. He saw the mountains, the waterfront, every leaf on every tree. The raindrops pounded down on him in a new way, mechanically,

unnaturally. It wasn't a natural rain. It seemed delib-
erate, the result of some decision.

It's raining for me.

The whole island was shrouded in mist, steaming
as if it had been doused with acid.

He lay down on his back. The raindrops fell into
his open eyes, and the precise rhythm of the pain they
caused was hypnotic. He entered a timeless space,
where everything was suddenly unbearably clear. The
earth breathed, the green of the leaves would have
blinded him if he'd looked, the houses on the waterfront were so white they would have burned his eyes
in an instant. This clarity threatened him from all
sides, all the more terrifying because it was something he couldn't grasp with his senses or his mind.
Some new thread now bound him to nature. But
without love, without ecstasy. He could no longer
understand anything, since he himself had become
raindrop, tree, soil, leaf, had become one with things
that were usually separate from him. But without
love. What he felt was disappointment. For a
moment he had believed he would see some vision,
hear some voice. But he felt neither joy nor sorrow.
There wasn't a single thought in his head. There was
no image, no sensation to help him understand, taste,
fear. Nothing was happening. And even now, as he
was living that nothing, he had already forgotten it,
since his capacity to remember had been wiped away.
Somewhere deep inside, though, in a place that

hadn't been touched by this death, he knew that this was only the first time, that there would be others, more violent, more complete. *I'm just an instrument.* He fell asleep.

When he woke, the rain had stopped.

The chief will be looking for me. He scrambled down the mountainside. At the station, the chief was distracted, busy with work.

"Listen, Manolis, you really have to stop eating at those souvlaki places. You should know better, we get complaints about them every day. Is your stomach feeling better?"

"I threw up."

22

They all saw it, but at first no one knew what it was. It was tiny, but it hit the wall with such force that they all flinched, as if to shield themselves. It fell belly-up on the ground. "The heat killed it," someone said. Mark picked it up and carefully stood it on its feet in the middle of the patio.

The bird stood there. Its eyes were open, but so still that it seemed to be sleepwalking. Mark said he hated birds, especially their eyes. The way they shifted their gaze from side to side so quickly, so nervously—it always seemed to him that they weren't just looking, but checking, trying to control. "I hate them," he said, "I hate them."

In the afternoon they always sat on the patio. Inside it was almost dark, they could barely make out Stephanos standing behind the bar. He was playing chess by himself, holding a lit candle in his hand. They always drank a lot in the afternoon, but never got very drunk. Perhaps because it was daytime and the bar was all theirs, with a kind of family atmosphere. Whereas at night, with the lights dimmed, surrounded by unfamiliar faces, they got drunk off their very first drink. And then there were the boys: so desirable, perched on high barstools with crew cuts and sunburned necks, rings in one ear, their tall, skinny, almost sickly bodies browned by the sun, pampered with oils and creams. It suddenly occurred to Mark that their eyes, darting to the right and left not to look but to check, were just like birds' eyes.

But now it was three in the afternoon and there were no boys to be seen. Just the bird standing petrified in the middle of the patio as they downed drink after drink and never got drunk. Sue suggested that someone bring water for the bird. "No, bread," Gunther said. Placido thought they should leave it alone. But they couldn't stop looking at it. Completely still, like a statue, it stared straight ahead at the mountain. Mark pushed a little plate of water up to its beak.

"I once had a lover who left me," Placido said. "All night I kept running and banging my head against the wall. He told me he was leaving because he was scared of spiders and had heard it was spider season. 'I'll buy you a mosquito net,' I told him, crying, 'I'll order nets for the whole house, I'll cover the garden, too, the whole island if that's what you want.' And you know what he said? That he was scared of mosquito nets, too, he was claustrophobic, and anyhow they were too expensive, and by the time they got here spider season would be over. I didn't love him, that's why I was so devastated when he left. All night I kept running and hitting my head against the wall, again and again. Toward morning, I stopped and stood dizzy and motionless in front of the mirror, I thought I was a bird. 'How can I fly away,' I kept saying, 'now that my wings are gone? How am I supposed to fly? How?'"

Mark kneeled and shook a few drops of water onto the bird's beak with his finger. The bird looked straight ahead, spitefully indifferent. Mark stroked it gently from head to tail. The bird shivered, not on the surface, but as if it something deep in its body were in spasms. He dripped water onto its head. The drops ran into the bird's eyes, trickling over its eyeballs. Everyone leaned forward, waiting for some sign of life.

"Fucking bird," murmured Sue.

"Hey, you guys!" Stephanos's voice sounded as if it were coming from the depths of some cave. "It's gin! The bird needs gin if it's going to fly."

"Don't we all?" Gunther replied.

Stephanos came out, staggering and planting kisses on a bottle of Gordon's. "You'll see," he said, "you'll see."

"No," Mark said. He kneeled and covered the bird with both hands. "He's mine to take care of."

"Nothing's yours anymore, nothing!" Stephanos was an angry drunk and he only got drunk in the afternoon. At night he had to be clear-headed for the customers. And Mark always made him angrier than the others. "You'll see," he told Mark, glaring at him, "you'll see, you'll see." He forced the bird's beak open and stuck a gin-wetted finger down its throat. The bird jumped back a step, then forward. Its eyes bulged. It started to look to the right and left, eyes shining; it seemed to be counting or measuring amazingly fast, and with a gaze both vacant and unbearably precise.

Mark stretched out his hand. With a movement even faster than the darting of its eyes, the bird turned and bit him, then spread its wings and was gone.

That evening at the bar, Mark sat beside to a boy with short hair, huge eyes, and small, childlike ears. The boy was slightly drunk. He was smiling, but his gaze was cold as he scanned the room. Mark suggested they go to his place for a drink, and the boy, throwing a final glance at the others in the bar, shrugged his shoulders and said, "Why not?" Toward morning, the boy asked for Brazilian coffee with brown sugar, then went and stood naked in front of the window, smoking as he looked out at the sky.

"You won't believe it," Mark told him, examining the boy's perfect back, the small hollows above his hips, "you won't believe it, but a bird bit me this afternoon."

23

It was almost noon. The harbor was packed. The *Eleni* was unloading bathtubs and cabinets, the tour boat had just docked and was letting out its Japanese tourists, the waterfront cafés were full.

"Ice cream!" Antonio called. Luka saw Manolis. He was walking toward her, smoking. A few minutes more and he would run right into her. Luka ducked into an alleyway. Manolis passed by, so close that his uniform almost brushed her arm. He didn't see her. He seemed tired, lost in thought. The bells of the cathedral rang twelve. Manolis vanished into the crowd.

24

They were dancing only tango. Luigi had thrown a party in honor of a dance troupe from Argentina. The stereo was playing "*A Fuego Lento*." Luka was watching one of the dancers. She liked his heavy eyelids—they hid a pensive, melancholy, moody gaze. He lit a cigarette, then returned her look.

She imagined herself in some brightly lit city, walking at night in black heels, a black skirt slit up the thigh, and a white shirt, completely naked underneath. She would wait at a red light, the cold air caressing her body. The dancer, sitting at a café across the street, would be watching her through the window, that pensive look in his eyes. She would cross the street, slowly swaying her hips just for him, her heels clicking on the pavement, and the dancer's face would draw near to the glass, aloof and desirable, as she passed directly before him, her chest firm, naked under her shirt, red from the cold. He would light a cigarette, and in the instant when his eyes were trained on the flame, she would turn a corner and disappear.

One of the girls from the troupe came up and asked her to dance.

"But I don't know how," Luka said. "I have no idea how to dance."

She glanced around the terrace. There were lots

of couples of women dancing. The sea shone in the distance. A boat passed by. There was a full moon. The women wore long, full skirts, were barefoot and practically naked on top.

The woman took Luka in her arms and they began to glide noiselessly over the white tiles. They danced all night without speaking a single word, to songs like "*Divina*," "*Amorpho Tango*," "*Nostalgias*," "*Canción Desesperada*." Toward morning, when all the other guests had left and Luigi had fallen asleep on the steps, the dancer left in the middle of a tango, without even saying goodbye. When she got home and took off her dress, Luka saw that the woman's hand had left a large red mark on her back.

25

The harbor was deserted. Luka saw him coming from far off. When he reached her, Manolis stopped. They looked at one another absentmindedly, as if they had never met. Then they kept walking.

26

Manolis stretched out on his bed. It was afternoon, he was tired, soon he would have to leave for the station. Usually he liked this time of day: he would eat standing up in the kitchen, then lie down with a cigarette in his mouth, hands behind his head. He would think. He never let himself daydream. He would take an idea and turn it over in his head for hours, directing its motion, not controlling it, just following it until he arrived at a solution. Sometimes he would fall asleep for a few seconds, a sweet sleep that left him more rested than the deep sleep of night. He never thought about the murders. He used the same knife to peel fruit or cut cheese, washing and drying it as carefully as he had cleaned it of blood. The murders weren't thoughts, they were actions, and by now they belonged to the world of daydream. They seemed so insignificant that several times he had almost confessed when he saw the police chief trying so hard to figure out who had committed the crimes.

He stretched out on the bed. He tried to find a thought to turn over in his mind. Nothing came. So he decided to think about that absence of thought. Today he was bored. His boredom intensified, spread out over the room. Now the room, too, gave off a sense of boredom, an ugliness. The walls, the chair, the table were reduced to shapes in space, meaning-less, functionless. On the wall by his head a black line of ants was crawling up toward the ceiling. He touched a finger to the wall. Then he drew an invis-ible circle, trapping them inside. They stopped abruptly and fell from the wall, landing dead on the floor. He went and got the broom and dustpan from the kitchen and swept up the ants. Then he combed his hair and left for the station.

27

The trash was piling up in the streets. Some of the islanders called the town hall to complain, and were told that the garbage man drank a lot and forgot to pick it up, or got the days confused. Everyone had always taken out their trash and left it on the corner by seven each morning, but now they let it go until later. Then they started taking it out any old time. They tossed it into the middle of the street, or dropped it off terraces and balconies. The kids had discovered a new toy. They rummaged through the bags and the girls made dolls out of chicken bones while the boys staged wars with the empty cans. One girl built a hospital out of eggshells. The trash bags started to form small mounds all over town. The narrowest streets were so full of garbage you couldn't get by. The whole town stank.

One morning people woke up to find themselves surrounded in trash. No one came to collect it anymore. Black bags blocked the roads, rising as high as the roofs. The sun beat down on them all day long, and at night the hot pavement warmed them from below. No one seemed to care. These days the only time the islanders left their houses was when they went out to throw more bags on the pile. It was as if they were trying all day to fill as many bags as they could, to bury the island in filth. As if they were eating ten times a day just so they would have more scraps to throw out. They dirtied the island maniacally, with the same passion with which they had once kept it clean. They had been overcome by a fervor for stench and pollution, a devotion as strong as the one that had once made them repaint their doors and whitewash their steps. They carried bags out and threw them blindly, not caring where they fell. The bags broke as they landed. Ants swarmed everywhere, dragging bits of trash. The streets flooded with rancid milk, rotten melons, empty cans. Despite the heat, the trash held its moisture, glued together by a thick, invisible mucus. The trash seemed alive, like a monster that had glutted itself and lay digesting in the sun.

One night, Manolis suddenly awoke. It was shortly before dawn. He leaned out the window. The stench hit him so hard it was like colliding with someone, body to body. The highest sack was close enough for him to touch, to plunge his fingers in. He hurriedly put on his uniform and ran out into the street, carefully smoothing his hair with his hands. "I have to be impeccable." Dirty water fell from above, staining his uniform, soiling his shoes. He heard a rustling behind him, turned and saw something run and hide in a sack, which started to tremble as if a scuffle were taking place inside. He reached the last of the narrow alleyways and tried to get across to the waterfront. The sacks were piled in the middle of the street like a barricade, the top of the heap disappearing into the night. He started to scramble over. He fell several times, plunging into mysterious sub-stances in various stages of decomposition. At some point he caught hold of something furry that struggled and thrashed. His panic turned to rage, his fear evaporated. He was gripped by a feverish impatience. "I'm going to clean it all up. I'll clean up the island, the world. If I don't do it, who will?" He stood for a moment at the highest point of the heap. Then he tumbled down the other side, landing on the waterfront.

At first he was confused. He didn't recognize anything. The trash that covered the wharf had utterly transformed its appearance. The bags rose in heaps, formed peaks and craters, turning the water-front into a moonscape. The black bags concealed the houses, all the way up to their roofs. The entire line of storefronts along the water seemed hidden behind a black mask. Manolis kneeled down amid rotten meat, moldy fruit, torn books. He grabbed an armful of trash, ran down, and threw it into the sea. Then another, and another. "Me," he said, "Me, me, me." He threw bag after bag into the sea. Faster, more violently, plunging his entire body into the trash. The water started to turn murky. A naked doll with yellow hair and a broken arm floated amid dirty papers. Empty cans jangled against the quay. One end of the wharf was slowly being cleared out. The sea beside it had turned hazy and thick. Manolis kept going, progressing methodically down the wharf.

Day was breaking. The light, like the water, was hazy and thick. In the middle of the harbor, Manolis took off his jacket and shirt and threw them into the sea. He had almost reached the last café, where the waterfront turned sharply and headed toward the row of cannons. Someone was sitting there, the table beside him covered with paints and brushes. It was Mark. He had set up an easel and was sitting with his back to the sea, studying the mountain of bags. He painted slowly, leaning his head back now and then to get a better view. Manolis watched him stand up, gather together a pile of trash, and arrange it carefully in front of the bags. "That'll help show how tall it is," Manolis heard him murmur. Mark was so absorbed in his work that he didn't notice Manolis, not even when he'd come so close that his naked chest was touching Mark's shirt.

"Are you crazy?" Manolis asked.

Mark looked at him without the least bit of surprise. "I knew you'd show up sooner or later. It's natural. This is a sight that could only interest you and me. You clean things up. I record. Good thing I beat you to it. I haven't touched this side yet. It's the most interesting. Over here the sacks have been piled in a particular way. They're all intact, perfectly assembled, like a Roman wall. The oldest bags are at the bottom. Above them, the ones that joined the wall later on. And on top, the most recent. Unless someone came along and secretly rebuilt the wall, switching the layers. Then the oldest would be on top. Of course we could tell by examining the degree of decomposition.

"I always dreamed of doing a series about garbage. Ever since I was a kid, trash has fascinated me. I remember, I used to sneak out of the house to pick through the garbage in the streets, I could look at it for hours. My first sketches, when I was seven years old, were of trash. I was already trying to capture its texture on paper. To express the organic relationship I saw arising between substances and materials that were so different from one another. How could this piece of fruit and this piece of meat, so distinct at home in our kitchen, take on another dimension as soon as they were both called trash, becoming parts of an indissoluble mass? For me it was pure metempsychosis. Decomposition became a kind of alchemy. And now here I am, on my knees in worship at the sight of this apocalypse. If you could only see the beauty in this scene, you'd stop cleaning, you'd stop throwing the trash in the water."

"But it's growing all on its own, it's gone wild. It's reproducing like crazy, like a disease."

Mark grabbed Manolis by the shoulders. "But look, just look! Don't you understand? Look!"

Manolis bowed his head. Then he went back to throwing trash into the sea.

The sun had risen. The sky was gray, dull. The air was so still the heat felt thick, congealed. Humidity drenched the pavement on the waterfront, keeping the garbage fresh and alive. It was flourishing. The bags, covered in dew, looked gray in that light, metallic. They had utterly destroyed the island. Everything was simmering, soaked, as if a secret distillation were taking place.

Mark painted. Every so often he would wipe away his sweat with the same cloth he used to clean his brushes. His whole body was dripping. He kept wiping his chest and neck. The cigarette dangling from his mouth got wet and went out. He chewed it, then swallowed. Behind him Manolis was out of breath. Mark listened to the sound of the water as the trash fell faster and faster into the sea. Manolis was crying and talking under his breath. The sentences were incoherent, disjointed: "I'm gathering things that can't be gathered. Am I blessed? I'll clean up the whole world. If I don't, who will? I'll never be able to understand your infinite perversion. First the murders, now this. Why choose me and not that one who's painting you, who understands your devious plans, and praises you for them? Whereas I don't understand anything, you chose someone who just executes your plans blindly, in ignorance. It must be part of your design. But why not him?"

Mark stood up. He put down his brush slowly, thoughtfully.

"What were you just saying, Manolis? Can you say it again? Who were you talking to?"

Manolis started in surprise. "Me? I didn't say anything. I thought you were talking. Strange stuff, gibberish."

Mark fell to his knees and threw his arms around Manolis's legs.

"What's wrong with you? Get up!" Manolis cried, pushing him. "Get up!"

Mark stood up slowly and lit a cigarette, looking down at the pavement. "That's how it should be, you not knowing a thing," he whispered. "But me, how could I not have realized? The signs were there from the beginning. It was written all over you. That's why I finished your portrait. I had to give a face to the one who has no name." He looked around. His voice was tired. "You're gathering the things that can't be gathered. Keep going, Manolis, do your job. It's too late now, but keep going." The sour stench of vomit came drifting over from the pile.

A cat dashed out of an alleyway onto the waterfront, chased by a pack of rats. There were so many of them that they bit one another as they ran, fighting to be first. When the cat reached the middle of the waterfront, it suddenly stopped. Motionless, the fur on its back raised, it stood on tiptoe, as if wearing heels. It stared hypnotized at the pack that surged around it, flooding the dock, as if caught in a headlight's glare. Its pupils were huge. It waited. The rats formed a large circle around it, then rose up on their haunches. They took their time, their movements slow and ritualistic. They were organizing a ritual, preparing a sacrifice according to inflexible rules. They communicated in high-pitched shrieks like the cries of newborn babies. It was as if the waterfront had filled with babies, crying out from within the heaped-up trash bags. The rats' circle tightened. They flared their nostrils, sniffing their victim. They moved even closer. They were walking on their hind legs, their bellies shining, fat and sleek, as if smeared with some rare ointment. They took a last step forward in unison.

The cat lashed out blindly. But the attack seemed purely for show, as if the cat didn't want to die without a fight against creatures it considered its inferiors. It disappeared beneath a black mass. The killing took place in absolute silence.

28

It was August 15, the day of the Assumption. The faithful swarmed toward the cathedral from all corners of the island for the evening service. The women's heels struck hurriedly against the cobblestones on the waterfront, sweat making their makeup run as they dragged their children in tow. The courtyard was packed. Those who couldn't get into the church waited outside for the procession, blocking the door, listening to the bishop over the loudspeaker. The icon was in the courtyard. It had been decorated with tiny white flowers and a single gardenia. The slanting rays of the sun lit up the silver offerings hanging on the icon and the gold behind the glass, hitting them so strongly that they seemed to be melting. You could barely see the Virgin's face. The members of the congregation looked at her with mistrust. They were used to seeing her in the half-dark of the church, and now, in the full light of the sun, they were bothered by how brightly she shone. Here they would never dare to bend and kiss her. Out here on display, she seemed almost indecent. The bishop was chanting, wiping the sweat from his face with a large silk handkerchief. "Hail, you who are highly favored, the Lord is with you…" His vestments were so heavy he could barely move. By the time he managed to raise his arms in order to emphasize some phrase, the phrase had come and gone, and he would be left standing there with his hands in the air, glowering at the crowd, trying to impart some mysterious meaning to his silence. The vestments were red, yellow, and gold. The red was of silk, light and shiny, but slightly dull, frayed from use. The yellow and the gold, both heavily embroidered, kept snagging on the soft red silk. This combination of fabrics gave the bishop an autocratic glow, which the strong red sun intensified, making the colors richer and deeper. Meanwhile, the varying lengths of his garments gave him a disorderly, modern air.

In the heat, the bishop exuded his own peculiar scent: something like patchouli, but mingled with another, mysterious odor that emanated from his garments, as if they had been drenched in litanies, liturgies, and processions dating back to Byzantium, and now those age-old odors, unchanged, flooded the churchyard anew.

The children snuck off and ran to the fountains. The boys filled their mouths with water and spat it out on the girls, who started to cry, since the water ruined the huge velvet bows in their hair. The bows fell forward, sopping wet, and dangled in front of their faces. The women had all doused themselves in hairspray, which smelled even more strongly in the heat, making everyone in the crowd sneeze. Some people complained, there were even grumblings about a new law: no hairspray in church, at least during summer. The younger women kept sneaking out the back to smoke, and whenever the bishop turned his head to glare at them, his beard would get caught in the heavy embroidery of his vestments. He kept an eye on the altar boys behind him, too, so they wouldn't talk. They were carrying large staffs topped with icons of the saints in golden suns. The boys snuck glances at one another, barely containing their laughter. The tips of their sneakers and a few inches of their jeans peeked out from beneath their silver and blue cassocks. Manolis was standing beside the icon with another officer. The two of them would be carrying it during the procession. Manolis was wearing a new uniform, was freshly shaven, and had gotten a haircut. He was staring hungrily at the icon. One of the men in the crowd noticed, leaned over, and whispered to his wife: "Good thing we've got him around. He's got morals. See how he's whispering along with the bishop? He knows the whole service by heart."

The altar boys swung their censers, the smell of incense mingled with the scent of the jasmine that climbed the walls and dropped its blossoms like ash onto the pavement. The heavy scent didn't diffuse in the air. It hung close to the ground, choking the crowd. The red rays of the sun beat down on the white courtyard, on the monks' cells that lined it, on the high white walls that enclosed the congregation. And all of that whiteness simmered and shimmered in the heat, misty and uncertain as a reflection. The incense, the perfume, and the utter absence of fresh air made everyone lightheaded, almost drunk. They laughed for no reason, spoke loudly, cuffed their children on the head. The women were all fanning themselves.

"Good thing there's not much trash in the churchyard," one woman said, sighing and holding a bottle of perfume up to her nose. A man standing behind her leaned over to reply, inhaled her hairspray, and sneezed.

"Can we please have some quiet!" the bishop intoned as if it were part of the liturgy. Wilting from the heat, the old women inside the church leaned against the standing pews. Their eyes were closed and they nodded at the bishop's words.

"… Rows of angels hail you, singing in harmony…" Two lines of sailors stood at ease. They were dressed all in white, with heavy black shoes and spats. The barrels of their guns were pointed to the floor, a sign of mourning for the Virgin.

The mules pounded the soil with their hooves. Recently they had been acting wild, and the islanders had shut them up in one of the ruins on top of the mountain, where the constant confinement had made them completely feral.

There was a sound of shattering rock and bone. A wall crumbled and fell, crashing down on one of the mules. The others trampled it, struggling frantically to reach the opening, using its belly as a springboard; their hooves and legs turned red, covered in blood up to the ankles. They squeezed themselves through the opening and ran.

"... Pure and holy Virgin, the crowds of angels in the skies and all the people on earth blessed your most holy passing..."

It was time for the procession. The two policemen lifted the icon onto their shoulders and stood at the front of the line. The bishop, altar boys, and sailors fell into place behind them, then the rest of the congregation. They started off. The churchbells rang out, in unison with the bells from churches all over the island. The people inside pushed and shoved as they exited the cathedral, trying to get a better view of the processional staffs, not wanting to miss any of the chants. They joined the crowd waiting outside. The women looked one another up and down, eyeing each other's Sunday best: flowered blouses, white pumps, the lace border on a slip, the pleats of a skirt. The men kept their eyes trained on the ground, and that bowing of their heads gave them an air of piety, though really they were just trying not to get their shoes dirty in the trash. Manolis felt the weight of the icon on his shoulder. He leaned his cheek against its gold frame and closed his eyes.

"... Hail, you who are highly favored, the Lord is with you, he who through you grants great mercy to the world..."

The icon glanced sideways, smiling at him. Silver offerings hung all around her head, her hands, her veil. Her face, smothered in jewels and trinkets, looked even sterner than usual, as if she didn't approve of the orgy of gold that crowded her on all sides. Rings, bracelets, exquisitely worked diamond brooches, little girls' earrings with blue stones, golden hearts, silver offerings in the shape of ears, hands, legs, eyes, livers, aortas, and other unrecognizable body parts hung in a confused mass, piled so densely that the Virgin seemed to be fighting to draw breath.

"... Blessed be the womb that bore Christ..."

The mules galloped wildly down the mountainside toward the town. Red hoofprints covered the first of the narrow streets. The mules ran, losing their way in the labyrinth of streets, passing the same spots again and again, painting the pavement with blood. They were drawn on by an insatiable desire to reach the sea. They went wild. Their hoofbeats shook the island. Finally they found the long set of stairs leading down to the harbor. They raised their heads, sniffed the salty air, and charged. The stairs were stained a thick red, as perfectly painted hoofprints multiplied on the stone.

"... And the frightful Seraphim..."

The crowd on the waterfront froze. A rumbling was coming from somewhere deep in the island. At first they thought it was thunder. When they felt the ground beneath them shaking, they thought it was an earthquake. Then they saw a black torrent rushing toward them, so fast they never even realized what was happening.

"... Arrange yourselves at the gates to welcome the bearer of the creator of heaven and earth..."

The mules charged. First the icon was knocked over and vanished from sight. Then everyone disappeared under the black bellies passing over them. There were cries and children's screams, but they were drowned out by the noise of running mules. Bodies exploded, limbs catapulted into the air, falling onto the trash, painting it red. The garbage seemed to be multiplying on its own, digesting the human flesh in order to speed its own decomposition, as if the new red mass that covered the wharf belonged to it. In a matter of minutes the trash had swallowed that mass and had once more conquered the waterfront. The scattered mounds of garbage came alive with the glistening sheen of fresh blood. The mountains of black bags were now red, blood sliding over the slick plastic, giving the bags a new face, both festive and terrifying.

There was a hand half-buried in the filth, a heavy ring with a seal on its pinky finger. Elsewhere, red toenails peeped out of a sandal. A head bobbed in the sea, bumping against the boats, its hair swaying in the bubbling red water.

The mules left the shapeless mass of victims behind and galloped up the road toward the cliffs. They ran with a new, uncontrollable fervor. They threw themselves forward, the tendons in their necks nearly snapping. They opened their mouths, closed their eyes, stretched their limbs in enormous strides. And then the mules turned into horses. As they galloped, their dull coats became shiny, their bristles shorter, silkier. Their limbs grew more elegant, long and slim. As they galloped, the true psalm rose from beneath their red hooves—the whole island became a church, and the sky its dome. They tossed their manes, their painted hooves pranced on the pavement with the charm and grace of dancers, leaving precise, glistening red marks behind, sketching a new island in blood. They ran. The red disk of the sun sank into the sea, and the red of the sea united with the red of the wharf. The island glowed feverishly. It seemed about to burst into flames like a volcano. The horses were on fire, too, galloping toward the sun. With each step they cut pieces of flesh from the burning light. They reached the edge of the cliff. Stretching their limbs exquisitely, they dove into nothingness.

Night rushed over the island, fell and covered it, blacker, denser than other nights. The mute masses of trash could no longer be seen, nor the bodies on the wharf. But in the still, heavy heat the odors were unbearable, especially the stench of blood. The whole island stank like a slaughterhouse. Blood was everywhere, black, invisible.

Manolis walked. The wharf was deserted, full of small rustlings. He couldn't believe that a few hours earlier the bishop had been chanting, the wharf had been full of churchgoers, and he, in a clean uniform, had been carrying the icon of the Virgin. Now he was almost naked, bruised and bleeding. He stepped in puddles of filthy water, searched under the corpses, plunged his hands into the blood and filth. He was looking for the icon. He went into the churchyard to rest. In the enclosed space the stench was overwhelming. He almost fainted. The garbage bags had inundated the churchyard too, as if they had moved there on their own. The stench throbbed around him like a living thing, reflected and strengthened by the white of the walls. It would kill him. He ran into the church to escape. He leaned against one of the standing pews, closed his eyes, and breathed deeply.

He couldn't see it yet, but he felt it. He heard the same rustlings of plastic, a whispering, and the dull, constant tremor of some strange growth. The church hummed like a factory. Manolis lit a candle and saw that the trash had risen as high as the dome; it filled the sanctuary, was heaped on the altar—not a single spot was untouched. And there, in its usual place next to the pews, was the icon. Manolis went up to the lectern by the sanctuary where the lead chanter usually stood. He stepped up and opened the hymnal. *Psalm Book, Liturgy of Baptism, Priest's Holy Prayer.* He started to read aloud. As he read his voice grew stronger, penetrating the walls of the church, covering the whole island, spreading over the sea.

"… And you, indescribable God, without beginning, expressionless, you came to earth, taking mortal form, born in the image of man…"

He raised his head, looked at the dome. An expressionless God looked back at him. Manolis squeezed his head between his hands. He was in intense pain, as if his brain were dripping blood. He looked again at the dome. God's mouth seemed to be steaming with vomit. Strange images filled Manolis's mind. He saw countless suns hiding the sky from view. He saw a field where grasses swayed and broke, everything else silent and still. He saw fish crawling from the sea to walk on dry land. Then he saw the sea receding and the island joining with the mainland in the distance. He looked again at the dome. His rage grew. He would have killed now, had there been a victim at hand, a victim chosen long ago, like the others. He stroked the knife hidden deep in his pocket—and as he had done during each of the murders, he suddenly broke into a cold, willing rage. He grabbed the lectern and smashed it with his bare hands. He dashed forward and overturned the altar, grabbed the double doors of the sanctuary, ripped them off their hinges, threw them to the ground and smashed them with his feet. He knocked over the stands of votive candles. He punched out the windows with his fist. The stained-glass angels shattered in the air and fell in shards to the floor. He ran up the winding staircase to the dome and tried to scrape off the paint with his nails, to ruin that face, disfigure it with scratches.

He ran back down and smashed all the pews that lined the walls, knocked down the icons. This new trash piled on top of the other, older trash.

Manolis went up to the Virgin. The glass case had been broken. Her silver offerings were now scattered in the trash. He took her in his arms, ran out of the church, rushed across the waterfront, and disappeared into the narrow streets of the town.

29

Mark wanted Dane. He had wanted him badly for a long time. Dane was practically a child. He looked like a wolf, or a weasel. He always showed up at the bar at around eight and left at dawn. He had slept with everyone, but always turned Mark down.

"I want to paint you."

"No," Dane would say, but then would give him an inviting look.

Dane always drank orange juice, never alcohol—"My parents won't let me," he said. Dane had become an obsession for Mark. Every night at the bar Mark would circle him like a dog as Dane drank orange juice and Mark got progressively more drunk, blind drunk, aggressive.

"Why with everyone else and not me?" he yelled.

"Because that's what I want," Dane would answer, sweetly and calmly. Dane drove everyone wild. Whoever slept with him once had to sleep with him again. It was strange, there were lots of other boys on the island. But Dane had a perfect combination of innocence and shamelessness. Dane was no play-thing, no object of others' desires. He chose his lovers. Dane was Dane.

One evening Mark was playing chess with Stephanos at the bar. It was ten and Dane still hadn't appeared.

"I took your rook, I took your knight, I took your queen—forget that asshole already," Stephanos said.

Dane showed up five minutes later. Mark lost his king, too. Dane didn't come in, just looked at Mark from the door. Mark knew that look, saw the smile that creased Dane's face, giving him that weaselish air. He went over to him.

"Let's go," Dane said. As soon as they were out in the street, Mark was all over him, trying to push him to the ground.

"No!" Dane said. "Can't you wait?" He smiled. "I've got other plans." He started to whistle, walking a few steps ahead, hands in his pockets. He kicked at a bag of trash. "I don't feel like being inside, with a bed and all that. Tonight I feel like soil and fresh air. Want to go up the mountain?"

Mark wanted Dane all to himself, cut off from any kind of distraction, in a prison cell with barred windows and nothing but a bed. Then he remembered Manolis's hiding place. Manolis was working the night shift, and no one else knew about the place. He had shown it only to Mark, and made him promise not to tell anyone else. But tonight the betrayal seemed trivial.

"Sure, let's go."

They scrambled up the mountain quickly, almost at a run. Mark lost all sense of time. He just stared through the darkness at Dane's scrawny body and listened to him whistling the same tune over and over. When they arrived Dane started jumping around excitedly. "This is exactly what I had in mind. Exactly." He threw off his clothes and started to dance. He suddenly seemed like such a child that his nakedness had no meaning, no significance, Mark even forgot why they had come. As he was dancing, Dane stepped on something strange, a spot that felt as if the ground below it were hollow. He bent down. "Mark! Mark! Come look!" They both kneeled on the ground, then pushed aside a thin layer of soil. Underneath was the stolen icon. It seemed as if someone had been covering it lightly with soil each day, so that he could uncover it quickly, impatient to look at it. The Virgin, on her back, half-buried, gazed up at Dane and Mark. She held Christ in her arms, and her veil had been soiled by the dirt. Dane lay down, covering the icon with his chest. He didn't move.

"I'm dead," he said, "I'm dead."

Then he stood up, and Mark saw that Dane had an erection. But the ecstasy that suffused his face made him look like an archangel. An archangel with an erection, wild and glorious.

Dane stood with one foot on either side of the icon and raised his hands in triumph. "Come here," he told Mark. "Kneel down. No, here. I want to be able to see her eyes." He put his hands on his hips and tossed his head back. Dane's penis thrilled Mark's mouth. Dane directed his movements, ordering him to touch him more gently with his tongue, or harder, further down. Then he grabbed the nape of Mark's neck and said, "Wait." Mark raised his eyes. Dane's head was sunk in darkness. His body stood out pure and clear in the night, like a blade, like a cross dividing the sky. Mark's eyes filled with tears.

"Lick," said Dane, then, "Wait." Mark stopped. He looked at Dane. Dane closed his eyes, concentrated, went soft. A torrent of urine hit the icon. An endless, transparent stream washed away the soil, until her eyes, her veil, her cheeks shone and her mouth grew wet. Dane stopped. Then he stroked himself with such familiarity and experience, such wisdom and knowledge, that his movements seemed almost pretentious. His erection returned. "Play with it. Just like I was doing. Forget I'm even here. Play with me the way you'd play with yourself if you were alone on the mountain fantasizing about me. It turns me on, that fantasy of absence, that's why I always close my eyes, so I can concentrate on that triumphant absence. It turns me on, because then any hand that touches me is my own." He kept talking as Mark stroked him, he didn't breathe heavily or moan, just swayed gently and spoke, directing Mark's motions— slower, faster, softer, harder, squeeze more, that's good, keep doing that, just that, don't stop. He was exacting and strict. "Wait," he said. He stood with his eyes closed, laughing softly at something that was entirely his own. Another few drops of urine trickled down the icon, and then, for the first time, Dane let out a moan.

Mark looked at the face above him, given over to profound pleasure, and felt jealous—he was just the middleman in some erotic act playing itself out both in front of him and somewhere else entirely.

"Stroke me," Dane said. "Wait." "Again." "Wait." The night split in two. The soil over the icon crunched. They had covered it almost completely, kicking soil onto it until all that showed was her eyes, which looked even brighter with the black soil around them, as if she were wearing makeup.

"Stop!" This time it was hard for Dane to keep himself in check. "Enough! Not here. I want to imagine all this later, when I'm alone."

"Come home with me and do whatever you want. I want to paint you lying in bed, imagining it all, I want to capture all the absences flickering across your face." Mark made a fist, as if grasping a brush. He imagined the painting. "You get turned on by the other's absence. But on the canvas, I'll be the one who makes you disappear. That's all I care about." He threw Dane's clothes at him. "Get dressed." Then he shoved him. "Hurry up. I want to draw you in lamplight. I always paint my boys at night."

When they reached his house, Mark got out the easel, the brushes, the paint.

"Do you have any coffee?" Dane asked.

"Shut up," said Mark.

"I want you now," Dane said. "I want you. Come to bed."

"Don't talk." Mark undressed him, lay him down, arranged him on the bed, turning on spotlights, orienting his legs toward one particular corner of the bed, turning his face to the light. Then he sat behind the easel, lit a cigarette, and picked up a brush.

"Now," he said, "get busy."

30

Luka was writing. The incredible heat and the stillness excited her. She wrote tirelessly. She had brought her things down into the dining room and was working at the table with the shutters half closed. Her papers were spread out everywhere: on the table, the sofa, the floor, even in the kitchen. She hadn't gone out in days. She slept, she woke up, she made coffee, she wrote. Her fever for the book rose with the temperature. She wrote physically, with her muscles, her whole body pushing the book toward its end. When she filled her pen she would wipe it off on her dress, on her legs, so she wouldn't have to get up. One day she noticed that the bottle of ink was almost empty. And this time it wasn't like those winter nights when she would come home from Anezoula's and drink down whatever was left. She laughed. "I've conquered the ink," she said aloud, and it felt like the biggest victory of all.

Luka didn't bother correcting her mistakes, she would do that later, at the end. For now she had to hurry. She had the feeling that there wasn't much time, and that feeling never left her for an instant. And so the book was drenched in a sense of urgency, a shortness of breath. Events, emotions, actions mingled exquisitely, blending together into a single shade. The heat, too, entered the book. In the final chapters the very letters on the page seemed to be boiling, scalding her hands. She didn't know why she felt this need to rush. All she knew was that Manolis was the one setting this frenzied pace, not only for her work but for everything around her. She worked day and night. She would sleep later. As she neared the end of the book, her love for Manolis swelled and grew. And she cried, because now she truly could have loved him. Now the time had come for them to meet. Yet she knew she would never see Manolis again, and that knowledge made her write with an even greater passion. She was trying to make him, like the words, pass through her body onto the page, so that she could forget him.

One morning the book was finished. The sun was unusually strong, closer than before. She put the book in a box and buried it in the garden, in the same spot where she had once buried her pen. She planted a flower to remind her where it was, a forget-me-not, one of few flowers that could survive the winter.

31

Since early morning the sun had been strong. But a light breeze was blowing off the sea and the air was clear. The humidity of the past few days had disappeared. The wind was dry, brisk. The town hall announced that a crew might be coming from the mainland that day to collect the trash. It had dried and withered. The blood had dried, too, and evaporated. Within a few hours, the sun had worked miracles. The villagers were cleaning their yards, whitewashing their steps. The cicadas were whirring again, and the sound marked the return to normalcy. The foul smells vanished. The stench from the garbage disappeared. The sun had disinfected the island.

Late in the afternoon Mark went down into the basement. It was the coolest part of the house. He used it as a cellar, and stored his wine there during the summer. Sometimes when he went down to get a bottle, he would stay and smoke a cigarette. After the blinding light of the rooms above, he found the half darkness and the absence of a view soothing. He sat on a bench and lit his cigarette. When he raised his eyes, he noticed the sun coming in through the skylight, which was as high and narrow as a well; it left a round, bright stain on the tiles. "I didn't know the sun ever came in here. I've never noticed before. But then there are lots of things I've never noticed."

It had been a while since he had last spoken to himself out loud. It felt strange. He only talked to himself in winter, to keep warm. And today, though the day kept getting hotter, he felt cold, he had the shivers, as if he were coming down with something. He thought of Dane, the floor upstairs around the bed covered in cigarette butts.

"And I gave the jerk three ashtrays."

He climbed the stairs with his bottles.

Down at the harbor, Antonio had stopped serving ice cream. No one wanted to eat in that heat, or even to drink anything but water. In the beginning, the waiter brought it in glasses, then in pitchers, then in old-fashioned jugs. Everyone laughed. They wanted to pay for the water, they said it would soon be as precious as gold, its price would shoot through the roof. They laughed, but kept throwing glances at the sun. At one point the waiter came out of the restaurant carrying a glass of water and raised his eyes to look at the sun. The glass fell from his hands and shattered on the ground. The water didn't even have a chance to evaporate: it simply disappeared, as if sucked in by some invisible mouth.

The disk of the sun whitened, as if its blood had evaporated in its own heat. The sky took on a thick, milky color. The line between the island and the sea became hazy, indistinct. The jasmine around the cathedral no longer had any scent. All the good smells had vanished, too.

Mark was working. Seated in front of the easel, he drank his wine slowly and painted. The sketch of Dane was becoming an oil painting. Paint covered the faint pencil lines, Dane's thighs came alive in all the shades of pink and brown. Mark removed all vulgarity from his slim, fragile, youthful body. Dane's portrait started to look like all the other headless portraits piled on the ground and covering the walls up to the ceiling. The heat suited them. They seemed to be sweating. In the furnace of that room, as the hours passed, their movements became more and more uncertain, more hesitant. One painting entered into the next, hands sunk in and touched the bodies beside them as the boys tried in vain to unite. But their mood wasn't erotic. They simply couldn't bear the solitude Mark had imposed on them when he imprisoned them, each alone in his painting. Mark was a little bit drunk. The wine and the heat aroused him, all his senses were sharpened. It had been a long time since he had concentrated so absolutely, and with such satisfaction, on his work. He hummed an old French song under his breath as he painted Dane's belly button carefully, using the tip of his brush to dab a little purple into that pink depression.

He went down to the basement for more wine. Standing at the door, his mood changed abruptly. A wave of fear rushed over him. Recently he had been having these attacks often. They always found him unprepared, they rushed through him like an electric discharge and left as fast as they had come. He had gotten used to them, he didn't pay them much attention anymore. He opened the door.

Something in the room wasn't right. He looked around. Everything was in its place, just as he had left it several hours earlier. He couldn't say why, but that sameness frightened him. It seemed superficial, unnatural, suspicious. The entire space had become a distraction, an illusion that kept him from identifying some awful aberration. A new wave of panic hit him in the stomach, his mouth filled with bile. His fear was protecting him, it was his body's last attempt to keep him from seeing. His muscles tensed, then started to twitch in uncontrollable spasms. It was like a physical stutter, as if his body couldn't control itself anymore, as if it could no longer keep pace with his thoughts. He doubled over. As he bent his head, he felt something burning the nape of his neck, so sharply he thought it was a bee sting. He raised his eyes, looked at the skylight. The sun was still falling straight into the basement, leaving the same big, round stain on the tiles.

The light beating down from the sky turned deadly. The change was sudden. The heat spiked, the temperature hit unprecedented heights. The stores and cafés closed. The island seemed deserted.

At Bill's they were dancing under the fans. Stephanos was playing chess by himself. He kept smearing vaseline into his cracked lips, and the chess pieces were all greasy. He had quit his job as barman an hour before, when, drunk, he had raised his eyes and seen the sun hanging suspended over the patio, ready to fall. Bill had looked up, too.

"Good for you, boy, I quit, too," he had said.

Now Stephanos was sprawled on the red cushions. "A vodka, please!" he kept shouting to whoever walked by. Everyone was serving themselves. They had stopped fixing cocktails and were drinking the liquor straight.

"Drink up, old chap! Good for the heat!" Bill kept saying, slapping them on the back.

They were all there. Sue, blind drunk, was performing a peculiar strip tease: she had started out naked and was slowly putting on Gunther's jeans and shirt. Gunther, meanwhile, was wearing her skirt, swaying to the music and slowly pulling the skirt down his thighs.

"I want to be a nigger! I want to be a nigger!" Sue howled.

"Baby, you are! Baby, you're as black as this fucking sun," Bill shouted, pointing at the sun. Sue looked at it and fainted. They lay her down on a table. Ron turned on the faucet to add some water to his whiskey. The water came out boiling, filled the bar with steam. It burned his hands and he started to cry. Stephanos hugged him and smoothed vaseline onto his burns.

Bill announced that he was going to shut the doors, "To keep out the beast!" He was the most sober of them all, and could see the heat lurking on the patio, ready to pounce. "Stephanos! The doors!"

Stephanos stood up, staggering, pulled the glass doors shut, locked them and put the key in his pocket. Then he went back to his chess game. In the closed space, the fans creaked unbearably, the music was deafening. They were dancing naked, frantic from the heat. Sue had fallen off the table and they kept stepping on her, until her body was covered with bruises. They grabbed liquor off the shelves and drank straight from the bottles. The gin, whiskey, and tequila steamed, burning their eyes and cheeks. When the power went off, they didn't realize right away. Their voices were louder than the music, and when it stopped they didn't even notice. But then they saw the fans spinning more and more slowly, creaking one last time and then coming to a stop.

"Stephanos! The key!" someone shouted. But no one moved. Stephanos, alone in his corner, absorbed in his game, didn't hear. "Checkmate!" he announced, then fell senseless onto the board. The pieces scattered over the floor.

To the others, who were in the final stages of intoxication, that movement, endlessly repeated in the mirrors behind Stephanos, seemed slow, unending, like the frame of a movie which the power outage had also stopped. The entire bar was cut off violently from the outside world.

Inside, noses pressed to the glass, they opened and closed their mouths silently, like fish in a tank. Their arms, sliding over the locked doors, looked like fins. The lack of oxygen distorted their features, made their eyes bulge—and yet from the outside it looked as if they were having the time of their lives, still singing at the top of their lungs.

The heat stole in, spread over the floor, and started to rise.

Now there were ghosts in the streets: the few people who still dared to go outside covered their heads with damp towels, even sheets, and ran for their lives. Others could stand the heat better, and went out with their heads uncovered, walked down to the harbor, and waited for something to happen. They stared in the direction of the sun.

"When do you think it'll set?"

"Shouldn't it be lower in the sky?"

"No, it's the longest day of the year. It's just moving really slowly."

"But I'm telling you, it hasn't budged in hours."

"Are you crazy? How can the sun just stop moving?"

"It's not setting, get it? How else can I put it? That bastard's not setting!"

The others attacked the man who had spoken last. Two nurses passed before them at a run, carrying a stretcher. A old man lay on it, opening and closing his mouth.

"What's wrong with him?"

"Dehydration! The hospital's full. We're out of drips."

"Use retsina!"

The nurses laughed. The others lit cigarettes. They liked this dehydration thing. This sense that there was an emergency, the embattled atmosphere, took their minds off something else, some vague but insistent fear.

The island, the sky, the sea all went completely white. The disk of the sun, directly above the island, sent out waves of heat that got stronger and stronger, and more frequent, like gigantic spasms. Snakes came out of their holes on the mountain and started slithering down toward the town in search of water. Adders slipped into cellars. Spiders and scorpions crept out of dried-up drains and hid under beds.

In the harbor, fish leaped into the air as if scalded by the sea. Whole schools of fish flew from the waves, tracing enormous arcs in the air. Some even reached the wharf, where they fell in twitching heaps.

Slightly outside of town, a woman saw the sun reflected in her well. A few hours later she looked and saw it again. A third time, much later, she looked again. The sun was still there, in precisely the same spot.

Just then, Placido was walking past the hospital. He looked at front of the building and saw Alfredo, or Alfredo's ghost, standing at one of the windows. His face was made up and he was wearing a lace nightie over fake breasts. His hair hung in loose waves to his knees. He smiled at Placido invitingly, gesturing for him to come closer. Then his smile twisted into an awful grimace, crude and vulgar, with the same familiarity and complicity as when, that winter, he had switched off the light, slipped into the bed, and nestled against Placido's back. In the utter silence and stillness of the heat, Alfredo moved his lips almost imperceptibly, whispering:

"How about a siesta? We still have a little time."

To escape the terrifying mirage, Placido made the mistake of looking up at the sky. The sun burned his eyes instantly, and for good. He felt no pain—he just plunged, relieved, into darkness. It felt refreshing, cool and damp, like a cave. His head filled with the sounds of the sea; the night that surrounded him felt velvety, like a starry sky. He had never felt so at peace. Now that he could no longer see, the course of events unfolded clearly before him. It all seemed insignificant, unimportant. Alfredo had come to the island to die, for the sole purpose of appearing now in this hospital window and causing him to look at the sun. Placido understood other things, too, events from his childhood, desires, fears, urges that had gone unexplained until now. They seemed insignificant, too, now that the darkness illuminated them with such precision. He sat on a rock and groped in his pockets for his lighter and cigarettes.

Mark had closed the shutters all over the house. For hours he had been sitting in absolute darkness. By now he was sure it must be night. He went downstairs. When he opened the cellar door, the light was blinding. The sun was in exactly the same spot, directly above the skylight.

For the first time in his life he locked the door behind him on his way out of the house. The sun swirled around him like a whirlpool. The air felt hotter than fire. An instinct warned him not to lift his head, though at the same time he had an intense desire to look at the sun. His lips cracked, his tongue swelled. But the most surprising thing wasn't the heat, it was the sudden joy that washed over him. He hadn't felt this way since he was a child, when crazy, inexplicable waves of joy would knock the wind from him. Beneath this indescribable sun, he felt the same joy as back then, and understood that the circle was finally closing. He sighed with relief. The years of unhappiness—an artificial unhappiness he himself had created, to help him bear the boredom and loneliness—were ending, here and now. The years of passion, of creation, now struck him as funny. He felt as carefree and irresponsible as a child. In this strange sunlight, the world became dark and mysterious again. He had needed that light—a light which, rather than revealing, obscured forever the outline, the curves, the cavities of the universe, and made him realize how for years and years he had been painting a false nature: there were no seasons, no hours, day didn't give way to night, the light that had tortured him never changed.

No, he hadn't understood a thing.

The station was sweltering. The officers, naked from the waist up, kept emptying bottles of water over their heads. The chief was reading Cavafy. One of the officers stood behind him, pouring water onto his head, taking care not to let it drip into his eyes.

"Slower, Yannis, I want to enjoy it." The chief sighed. "This Cavafy guy is just awful. Where's the emotion? When I read I want to get a little bit bothered, a little bit upset. And all he seems to write about is sofas, lamps, mirrors. As for the infamous homosexuality, I don't see it anywhere. Every so often he thinks about some kid he knew in his youth. But I think about my nephew, what's the big deal? Anyhow, it's good reading for this heat, it calms me down. And I do want to educate myself. Besides, just imagine if I were reading something else, something that gets the blood pumping. I'd probably die on the spot!"

Mark came into the station. He sat down across from the chief, pulled a wilted cigarette from his pocket, and put it between his lips. The chief waited.

"I want to talk to you. But everyone else has to leave," Mark said.

The chief nodded almost imperceptibly. The others went out and closed the door behind them. When they were alone, Mark smiled at the chief almost tenderly.

"Now that you're on your own you're scared, huh? Don't be embarrassed, I'm scared shitless myself."

The chief waited. Today he didn't even notice how informally Mark was speaking to him, using the singular. Mark looked out the window. He spoke absentmindedly, the way he talked to himself at home.

"I came to turn Manolis in. He committed the murders and stole the icon."

The chief looked at him, astonished.

"Which Manolis are you talking about? Ours?"

"Yours, and mine."

"I don't believe you," said the chief.

"You don't have to. He confessed to me about the murders a long time ago. As for the icon, you'll find it buried in a clearing up on the mountain, behind the monastery. It's a place you don't know about. Manolis made me swear to keep it a secret. I found the icon there last night."

"What were you doing up there at night? Were you alone?"

"More or less," Mark said.

"And who's to say you didn't steal the icon? Or that you're not the murderer?"

"Idiot," Mark said. "For a long time now he's wanted you to arrest him. He told me himself, 'I'll confess as soon as they catch me. I want them to arrest me, I want it to be over.'"

"Do you have any ideas about his motivation?"

"Yes. But it doesn't concern you."

"Are there other crimes you're accusing him of?"

"Yes: he's not who he seems."

"What do you mean? He's using an assumed identity?"

"Yes."

"Do you know his real identity?"

"Yes. But that doesn't concern you, either. Just catch him for the murders and the icon. The rest is outside your jurisdiction."

The police chief stood up. He opened the door and looked at the officers standing in the hall. He tried to speak, but the anger and shock made him stutter.

"Manolis," he finally managed to spit out. "Bring him in."

The policemen poured out over the island. They started in the town. They went into houses and found people dying in their beds, watching TV. In the darkened rooms the image on the screen shimmered with heat. On the news someone was giving the weather report. All over town TVs were on, sounds from the same program floating out through the shutters. They searched the houses one by one. One of the policemen saw an old man fry two eggs directly on a marble tabletop, then dip his bread in the yolk. The policeman sat down on the front step of the man's house and started to cry. He told the others to leave him there, to go on without him—he had put up with it all, he said, but the sight of those eggs frying in that darkened room was too much. All he wanted was to die, if he could. Then he started to laugh, and said he was going to go back in and help the old man fry up some potatoes to go with his eggs. The others left him there, headed out of town, and started to climb.

Up on the mountain, the heat had withered the leaves on the trees. It had pushed its way deep into the earth, sucking up the moisture, drying out the soil. It drifted low over the island like a huge winged shadow, scorching everything as it passed. The policemen knew the terrain well. They searched every gorge, every cave, all the cells in the monastery, they broke open locked doors, lowered themselves into cisterns. Manolis was nowhere to be found. They kept climbing up the mountain. One of them fainted and the others kept going without him. At last they reached the clearing. When they saw the icon half buried in the soil, they sensed Manolis's presence nearby. The paint on the icon had melted. Rivulets of green ran from the corners of the Virgin's eyes, coursing down her cheeks. She had been blinded by the heat; she had been transformed. Red paint from her mouth flowed down her neck and chest, soiling her veil with blood. The colors merged and her face seemed to twitch, changing expression, metamorphosing with nightmarish speed. None of them dared pick her up. They also didn't dare turn their backs on her, leaving her uncovered like that. They threw on more dirt until she was completely buried.

They reached a cluster of ruins at the top of the mountain. Again they sensed Manolis's presence. They looked in vain for some shade where they could sit and rest their eyes. They tried to spit into their palms to wet their foreheads, and found that all their saliva was gone. They lay down on the ground, and the hallucinations began. Half blind, they saw figures passing before them, and each time they thought it was Manolis. One man even insisted he could smell Manolis smoking, the distinct odor of Camels. They heard barking. A pack of dogs ran through the ruins. The trough they usually drank from was dry. The dogs licked at the hot, dry stone, searching for a drop of water. Then they started to bark, sending the message on in high, hysterical cries. The hot earth scorched their paws and they jumped and danced. As their thirst grew they began to bite one another, trying to quench their thirst with blood.

Mark was sitting at the Hydronetta. He had chosen the best table, at the edge of the cliff. His feet dangled in nothingness. He was thirsty. He went into the café. The heat had burst the bottles, the floor was covered in shards of glass. He turned on the faucet but no water came out. The espresso machine was broken. The water had evaporated, the pipes were rusted, the machine looked as if it hadn't been used in years. He went back outside, searched his pockets for his cigarettes, and found that he had none. The ground was littered with cigarette butts. He started to pick them up, until he had filled both his pockets. Then he sat back down and arranged them carefully on the table, the biggest on the left, the smallest on the right, the same way he ordered his brushes. He would smoke the small ones first and save the big ones for last. "It's morning. It's morning and I have to get up, have to pretend I'm opening my eyes, stretching, smiling cleverly at the thought of my work, brushing my teeth, making coffee." Those words belonged to his winter ritual. "What made me think of that now?" The cigarette butts lying on the table made him feel more alone than the empty island had done. He started to cry silently. The tears fell into his open palms, and he licked the drops. "I never would have guessed that one day my own tears would grant me a few more hours of life." He tried to cry harder, but that struck him as funny, and suddenly he felt better. He lit the first of the cigarette butts, took off his shirt, put on his sunglasses, and leaned back in the canvas chair. "I'll get a tan. For the first time in my life I'll get a tan."

Mark was short, shriveled, as small as a child. His hair, once blond, had started graying years ago and had ended up a dirty yellow color. His face was covered with wrinkles, like a monkey's. And as with monkeys, the countless lines that criss-crossed his face gave it an almost fluid appearance, like the surface of a liquid constantly furrowed by the breeze. The smallest spasm could destroy it completely, alter its structure, its architecture. His face didn't change expressions, things just shifted around, like a moving stage set where props are forever being added or taken away, the space continually being transformed. Mark's face was a stage crowded with props, or a painting in which each figure, absorbed in its role, ignores the figure beside it, and together they comprise a complex and futile whole. His eyes were a light, faded blue. No one could bear Mark's gaze, not even Mark himself. Once he had tried to paint a self-portrait from his reflection in the mirror. When he got to the eyes, he gave up. The mixture of pain and irony he saw there frightened him. Because he could see that the irony wasn't there to hide the pain. On the contrary, the pain was just a distraction, something intended to conceal his deeper, ironic nature. Since that day, he had never once looked in a mirror. He had always worn sunglasses, even at night, sometimes while he slept. Only with Manolis had he taken them off. Now, sitting there, he suddenly knew he would never see Manolis again. Not because Mark was dying, but because Manolis's time had passed. When he had first seen Manolis on the day of the Carnival parade, he had thought, *Now the time has come for this person to exist.* And now the time had come to say goodbye. Mark felt nostalgic for Manolis. He felt nostalgic for his house, too, and for a certain white mug with blue flowers that he had left beside the easel, a mug he had always hated.

He looked down at his body. His skin wasn't peeling, it had come loose altogether, leaving his fatty flesh uncovered. The sun penetrated him with masterly strokes. He felt as if his entire body were on fire. His arms, his hands, his neck, his chest, his belly all became flames of pleasure. He was ready. At the final moment, he threw his sunglasses over the cliff, raised his head, and looked directly into the sun. "At last," he said.

The island wasn't scared anymore. It gave itself to the sun, opening like a body. No one would tire it anymore, no one would hurt it by looking at it or stepping on it. Its shape was clearly outlined: a naked black rock, and in the middle of the coast, the town, a small, dazzling white petal surrounded by the black of the island. The houses, built into the slope of the mountain, tumbled down to the waterfront with incredible joy. From above, the town looked like a white bird that had just touched down on the earth and was about to take off again. And everywhere, the rocks, the cliffs. They sank into the sea, making the water sparkle brilliantly with metallic gleams, creating a second island beneath the waves, a reflection of the one above.

The island had never been so beautiful, utterly revealed by the sun. Silence became sound.

It was a perfect day. At Antonio's, faded red chairs filled the wharf. Outside the boutiques hung dresses, shirts, racks of plastic beach shoes. The bakery door was open. In the marketplace, crates were laid out on the tables, baskets piled inside the shops, scales hanging empty and ready. Further down, the police station and the hospital looked like hotels, their doors wide open. The patio at Bill's was ready for business, umbrellas open over the white tables, flowerpots waiting in a row. At the movie theater by the harbor, glossy pictures advertised the evening show: a woman was kissing three different men, making sure they didn't mess up her hair.

It was a perfect summer day, and the sun shone motionless in the sky.

Translator's Note and Acknowledgments

Almost always with modern Greek literature, the translator must negotiate between the shifting linguistic levels created by the long and complex history of the language. *The Sleepwalker* throws another wrench in the works: the frequent occurrence of phrases, even entire sentences, in languages other than Greek. This, too, is a fairly common problem, since many speakers and writers of Greek are multilingual, and are accustomed to drawing on other languages in their conversation and prose. In *The Sleepwalker*, however, many of the characters are themselves foreign, and writers or storytellers to boot. What one character calls "this problem of languages" thus becomes one of the central axes of the novel. In translating, I have tried to make the reader aware of Karapanou's astonishing yet rarely estranging mishmash of languages—English, French, German, Ancient, Biblical, and Byzantine Greek, the halting Greek of ex-pats and tourists, and of course the starkly beautiful Greek of her own prose— primarily in order to underline the novel's preoccupation not just with langua*ges* but with language, and the problems of narrative and communication that underwrite it.

As always, I thank David, Helen, and Michael Emmerich for reading multiple drafts of this translation over the course of several years. I also thank Hilary Plum and Pam Thompson at Clockroot Books for their careful editing, and for trying to give Margarita Karapanou the readership in English she so richly deserves. I would like to dedicate this translation to the memory of Stefanos Tsigrimanis, who was always unfailingly generous with his help on this and other projects, and whose zest and brilliance will be missed by many.

—Karen Emmerich